Welcome to Shady Gulch, Dakota Territory.

Silver Dollar Saloon

Savannah

Lottie Mae

LOTTIE MAE

Silver Dollar Saloon

Paty Jager

Windtree Press
Hillsboro, OR

This is a work of fiction, Names, characters, places, and incidents either are the product of the author's imagination or are used fictitiously, and any resemblance to actual persons living or dead, business establishments, events, or locales, is entirely coincidental.

LOTTIE MAE: SILVER DOLLAR SALOON

Copyright © 2018 Patricia Jager

Contact Information: info@windtreepress.com

Windtree Press
Hillsboro, Oregon
http://windtreepress.com

Cover Art by Christina Keerins
CoveredbyCLKeerins

Published in the United States of America

ISBN 9781947983670

Disclaimer

Shady Gulch is not a real town in North Dakota nor was it a town in the Dakota Territory at the time of this book. I took information about railroad towns along the Northern Pacific Railroad and made my own town and populated it with the ethnic groups that traveled to the area to start new lives.

Special Thanks

Thank you to Marcia Montoya for beta reading and to Dalice Peterson for making sure my stories sparkle!

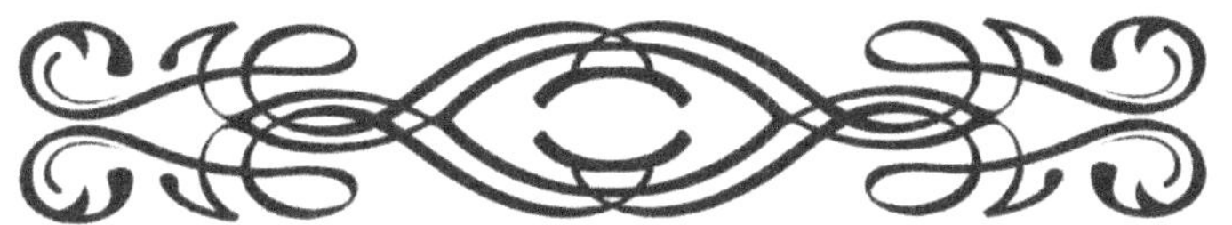

Chapter One

Shady Gulch, Dakota Territory
1879

Lottie Mae Peck was drawn to the conversation at the table by the door of the Silver Dollar Saloon. Manfred Albrecht, the blacksmith and part-time bouncer for the Silver Dollar, looked frustrated as he talked and drew on a piece of paper.

The railroad man who had walked in with Manfred seemed frustrated as well. He'd been asking if the blacksmith could make something for the train engine. Lottie Mae had heard others, who'd entered the saloon, talking about how the train had broken down a few miles out of town.

She leaned over the table, placing the beers the railroad man had ordered in front of both men. A glimpse of the drawing and she understood what the man was trying to ask Manfred.

"Manfred," she said, catching his attention.

The large man shifted, peering into her face. "Ja, Miss Lottie?"

She grasped the pencil and drew lines on the drawing. "This is what is broken. I know you can fix it." She smiled at him.

His eyes lit up, and he slapped his hand on the table. "Ja, I can fix train," he said to the man. "And I have the iron." He stood. "I get wagon. Go to train."

"Good. Good." The railroad man smiled at Lottie. "Thank you, young lady. I wasn't making myself clear."

Manfred was already out the door.

"His English is getting better, but he doesn't always understand new words." And she was getting a good idea of how to help him with that.

The railroad man handed her a silver dollar. "Thank you. You saved me having to go all the way to Bismarck to find someone to fix the train."

She attempted to give the man back his money.

"You keep it," he insisted as he walked out the door.

Lottie Mae walked over to the bar, staring at the silver dollar.

"What did you do that sent Manfred out of here like his pants were on fire?" asked Beau, the owner of the saloon, and the benefactor of all the women who worked in the saloon and stayed in his boarding house.

"I helped him understand what the railroad man wanted him to do." She flipped the coin. "And look what the railroad man gave me."

Beau smiled. "I told you, you should go back to teaching. You're a natural."

Just the thought of stepping into a classroom after

what had happened to her, made her teeth grind and her fists clench. "I don't plan to step in a school again. Not until I'm old and fat." She was working in the saloon because her family, her superintendent, and the whole community turned on her when she'd been raped by three of the older boys she'd taught. No, she'd not go through that humiliation again.

She put the silver dollar in the pocket of her dress and tapped the top of the bar. "I'm going to supper."

"It's early." He studied her.

The bad thing about being picked up out of the gutter by her boss, he knew everything about her and could tell when she was upset.

She glanced at him over her shoulder as she entered the store room. "I need a change of scenery." She winked and walked straight through the storage room, out the back door, across the alley, and into the kitchen of the boarding house run by Mrs. Dearling.

The woman would wonder why she came to supper so early but wouldn't ask questions. Mrs. Dearling was strict about men other than Beau, Jules, co-owner of the Silver Dollar Saloon, Reverend Webster, and the doctor coming into the boarding house. She also made sure no other men were allowed in the parlor without her being present. She said it was how they made sure the townsfolk knew the girls were women of moral integrity.

Lottie Mae wasn't really hungry. She'd had an idea and wanted to think it through without the noise of the saloon. She went straight up to her room on the second floor and closed the door. Teaching had been all she'd wanted to do from the moment she'd opened a book and learned the letters could be arranged into words and stories could be told. But the event that landed her here in Shady Gulch working for Beau Gentry had soured her on ever stepping into a classroom.

However, she could help Manfred learn to read, write, and understand English better. She sat on her bed, thinking up a way to approach him about the possibility. She pulled the silver dollar from her pocket. She could purchase a reading book, tablet, pencil, and slate for him. And they could spend an hour a morning together before he opened his blacksmith shop.

She just had to convince him it was a good idea. Happy at the thought of teaching someone and spending time with Manfred, she stood up, and smoothed out her saloon skirt that came to her knees. A quick peek in the mirror ensured her hair hadn't fallen out of the bun she'd put it in before going to the saloon. The red locks were all pinned in place. She tugged up on the bodice of the dress. While Beau didn't allow them to dress as skimpy as most saloon girls did, she still didn't like the fact so much of her chest showed.

When she'd been ostracized in her community, they'd said she'd lured the boys into their behavior because of her clothing. She had worn a summer dress which had a lower neckline, much like the one she wore now. What a woman wore shouldn't be a flag to a male to take a woman the way those three had. Her body shook, and her breathing quickened remembering the attack. She'd never been so frightened or devastated. They'd left her in the bushes behind the school, crying, her skirt up over her head as they'd walked off laughing.

Her stomach lurched at the memory. She grabbed

the chamber pot and retched into it.

This had to stop. Every time she dragged that evening up, this happened. She was the tough one in this house. She stood up to men at the saloon, knowing Beau and Jules had her back. This weakness angered her.

"Lottie Mae?" Freedom asked, knocking on her door.

"Yes," she croaked and swallowed to ease the tightness in her throat.

"Are you alright? Mrs. Dearling said she hadn't seen you." Freedom opened the door. Her gaze landed on the chamber pot still in Lottie Mae's hands. "Sugar, you have to move on." The negro woman her own age, hurried into the room and eased the chamber pot away from her. "What brought this on? Nothing in the saloon that I could tell."

Freedom placed the pot back where it belonged and sat on the bed beside her. "You need to look forward, not back. Beau said you were to come back to work when I came in for supper."

Lottie Mae nodded. He thought she'd been over here eating. "I'll grab a roll and head over." She shot to her feet.

"No, you won't. You'll come on down to the kitchen and eat something easy on your belly." Freedom stood and walked over to her. "We all wish our pasts had been different. The only way I keep from doing that, is by looking forward and not back. If I brought up memories, I'd never be able to get out of bed in the morning."

Lottie Mae nodded. She rarely thought about that

evening. But when she did… "Let's get supper and get back to the saloon." Though they worked long hours and were on their feet most of them, it was worth it to be so tired when she went to bed that she didn't have time to think about what put her here.

They walked down the stairs. Mrs. Dearling met them at the kitchen doorway. "My heavens, Lottie Mae, I didn't know you had snuck in here. Come, sit down and fortify yourselves for the evening."

Lottie Mae sat down in her usual place alongside Freedom and forced down the bread, cold meat, and preserves. Of all the women living here and working in the saloon, she was the one with an ample bosom and hips. And the one most of the patrons of the saloon ogled. She liked the nights she worked behind the bar. Most of her attributes were hidden.

"I heard you helped Manfred this afternoon," Freedom said.

"He was having trouble understanding what the railroad man wanted him to do." Thinking about helping Manfred pushed away her sad thoughts.

"I'm sure he'll do a good job for them. Everyone who comes into the saloon talks about what a good blacksmith he is and we're lucky he settled here." Freedom picked up her glass of water and drank.

"Dr. Nolan said the other day that Manfred fixed his buggy to better than new," Mrs. Dearling added.

Lottie Mae studied the two women. Why were they gushing about Manfred? They both had a gleam in their eyes that looked like they were being matchmakers. She liked Manfred. He was a big man, but he had a gentleness to him that appealed to her.

"I'm heading back to the saloon." She drank the

rest of her water and stood.

"I'll be right there," Freedom said.

Lottie Mae left through the back door. She made a stop at the outhouse and entered the saloon through the storage room. Even though she'd been skeptical when Beau found her and gave her a job at the Silver Dollar, she loved all the people who worked in the establishment like family.

The yeasty scent of beer in the storage room disappeared as she walked into the low hanging smoke in the saloon. Another evening of serving drinks, dancing, and paying for her room at the boarding house.

Chapter Two

Manfred stood outside the Silver Dollar Saloon debating if he should bother Miss Lottie now, while she worked. The railroad man had paid him twice what he'd usually get for the same type of work. If not for Lottie Mae helping him understand the problem, he might have lost the job.

"What are you doing standing out here, Manfred?" Sheriff Blake asked, slapping him on the back.

"Talking to myself," he said, with a weak smile.

"Come on, I'll walk in with you." Sheriff Blake opened the door of the Silver Dollar and motioned for him to walk through.

He liked this door, it was one of a few in this town that he didn't have to duck to walk through. Being nearly seven feet tall had its draw backs. But it also intimidated people without him having to be tough.

The second he stepped into the smoky bar his gaze

found Miss Lottie. She was working behind the bar tonight and the saloon was packed. He'd have to shoulder his way in between men if he wanted to speak with her. And then everyone would hear what he said.

He frowned and stepped to the side to allow the sheriff entry as he debated what to do.

Beau, the owner of the saloon, beckoned him to the far end of the bar.

Manfred walked across the room, aware he was being watched. He'd helped out a few times as the bouncer while Beau and Jules were away. Talking with Miss Lottie had been easy then. They were both doing their jobs, keeping the saloon running.

"Here, take this spot at the end of the bar," Beau said, placing a glass of foaming beer in front of him.

Manfred stood at the bar which came mid-chest on most men and hit him at his waist.

"Did you get the job finished for the railroad?" Beau asked as he poured drinks.

"Ja. They paid me good. I wanted to thank Miss Lottie for helping me understand." He raised the beer to his lips as his gaze watched Lottie smile at the men at the bar. He'd noticed her smile didn't light up her eyes when she worked in here. Only when she talked with him, Beau, Jules, or the other *frau.*

Beau nodded toward Lottie. "She was a teacher before she came here. You might ask her to help you with your English."

"Ja? A teacher?" That explained why she helped him understand so easily. He liked the idea of being alone with Lottie and having her help him with his words.

"A good one," Beau added.

Manfred studied him. "Why does she work here instead of at the school?"

Beau's eyes flared in anger before they softened with sadness. "It's a story she'll have to tell you in her own time. Be patient for the answer, her past is something she'd rather forget."

Manfred nodded. He had a past he wished didn't haunt him most nights. Yes, he knew all about trying to forget your past.

"I'll trade ends with her and you can talk." Beau wandered down the bar, said something to Lottie that shot her gaze to him. She nodded and made her way down the bar.

"Evening, Manfred," she said, tilting her head back to peer up at him.

"Miss Lottie." He smiled. "Thank you for your help today. I made more money than I could imagine. Mr. Parker told me he would send more work my way. He said I was aptly suited for being a blacksmith." He frowned. "I do not understand, but he smiled when he said it."

She smiled. This time her eyes lit up and her cheeks darkened a bit. "He said you are 'aptly suited' meaning you are big and strong and can pound out metal faster and better than others. That is why he wants to send you more work."

He grinned. "Ja, I can forge a wagon spring faster than anyone." Bragging was not his usual way. "I'm sorry, I did not mean to *damit angeben.*"

"To what?" Her pretty face wrinkled around her eyes as she thought.

"To talk about myself. Make myself important."

"Oh, to brag." She smiled. "You weren't bragging, you were telling the truth."

"Can I get another beer if you're done flirting?" one of the men three down from him asked in a surly manner.

"Be right back." Lottie grabbed the man's beer glass and filled it from a barrel behind the bar.

He had hauled in several of those for Lottie when Beau was gone. Watching her work, he didn't like her in here. She should be in a school room as Beau had suggested. Maybe he could pay her enough to teach him, she could stop working in the saloon.

She filled several more beer glasses and poured more whiskey into the small glasses before returning to the end of the bar. "The men are thirsty tonight," she said.

"Summer does that to a man. The heat and wind here is harsh." He took a long draw from his beer glass.

"Are harsh. You used heat and wind, that's two things. The sentence is; the heat and wind are harsh." Her cheeks darkened, hiding the faint freckles on her face.

"Thank you. That is twice today you help me with my English." He inhaled, fortified his confidence and asked, "Would you teach me to talk better English? Maybe even write? I would like to write down the work I do and the money I ask."

Lottie shot a glance toward Beau whose attention was on a story being told at the far end.

Manfred cleared his throat, drawing the woman's attention back to him. "I can pay you."

She shook her head, and his stomach dropped to

his knees. He should have known she wouldn't want to waste her time trying to teach him anything.

"You don't have to pay me. I'd be honored to help you understand English better." Her gaze met his and his heart soared.

"Really? You would help this *dummkopf* German?" He couldn't hide the happiness forming his words.

She smiled back at him with what felt like the same intense happiness. "Yes. I think it would be fun to help you."

He slapped his hand on the counter.

The loud slap captured everyone's attention, and the silence afterward made his words, "When do we start?" ring throughout the saloon.

His face flamed with embarrassment.

"What are you two starting?" someone hollered.

That caused Lottie's face to darken.

"Nothing that concerns any of you drunks," Beau said in his deep booming voice.

Jules began playing a song and Freedom, the dark-skinned saloon girl, sang.

Everyone's attention turned to the stage, and Manfred leaned down so he didn't have to talk loudly, "Can you come to the blacksmith shop tomorrow at nine?"

"I'll be there," Lottie said, before moving down to the other end of the bar and sending Beau back.

Manfred didn't know if she left because they'd concluded business or to keep people from talking. He hoped it was the later. Their schooling was a wonderful way for him to get to know Lottie better.

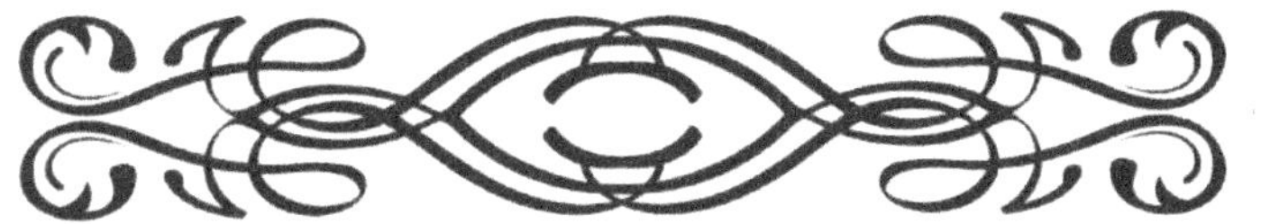

Chapter Three

Lottie Mae didn't usually get up this early after working the night before at the Silver Dollar, but she was excited to teach, even if it was to one person. She thought of how kind the blacksmith was and how he had become as embarrassed as she had when he'd smacked the bar and caught everyone's attention.

She giggled as she pulled up the front of her hair with combs and let the rest hang down her back. It had been years since she'd felt this lighthearted. The dark green skirt and calico bodice were her best everyday clothes. If she dressed in anything nicer everyone would think she liked Manfred. Her heart picked up speed thinking about how his size didn't scare her because he was so gentle. So different from any man she'd ever met.

Making sure the silver dollar from the railroad man

was in her skirt pocket, she headed down to get something to eat before going to the mercantile to purchase the items they would need to start Manfred's lessons.

"Heavens, you're up early this morning, Lottie Mae." Mrs. Dearling bustled about making breakfast for Beau, Jules, and the ladies when they all arrived in the kitchen at ten. Working until two in the morning, made it hard to get up any earlier than nine, usually. If she kept teaching Manfred, she'd have to get up this early every day.

"I'm helping Mr. Albrecht learn better English. He wants to be able to read and write it as well as speak." She sat down as Mrs. Dearling, the mother figure in the boarding house, placed fresh bread and chokecherry preserves on the table in front of her.

"I don't have anything else prepared," the woman apologized.

"This is all my stomach wants with so little sleep." Lottie Mae smiled at the woman and spread the preserves on her bread.

The smell of the fresh baked bread filled the kitchen along with the heat. Mrs. Dearling rose early during the summer to get the baking and cooking done to keep the house bearable to sleep in at night. But she also knew these days took a toll on the older woman.

"You and Beau should have asked Dallie to continue working here a couple days a week after she and Eldon married." Lottie Mae knew Dallie was bored being a housewife. Eldon had found a job with Judd Campbell at the grain elevator. Which left Dallie with very little to do with her day after cleaning and doing laundry once a week. When the young woman had stayed at the boarding house after Beau saved her from a life in a brothel, she'd helped Mrs. Dearling with all the household chores.

"She's a newlywed and needs to learn to take care of her home proper." Mrs. Dearling kept up a strong front, but they all knew she had less and less energy to run the boarding house.

Lottie Mae decided she'd make a point of bringing up Dallie helping out to Beau. She was sure he'd agree and make Mrs. Dearling see it was good for everyone.

Her breakfast eaten and washed down with a glass of water, she wiped her mouth, and grabbed the bonnet she'd placed on the chair beside her. With the bonnet in place, she hugged Mrs. Dearling and left the boarding house by the front door.

When she wasn't going to work at the saloon, she used the front door for entering and leaving the boarding house. It made her feel like it was filled with young women who had respectable jobs. While each one of them would never wish to go back to the life that brought them to Beau and the Silver Dollar Saloon, most yearned for the day they could marry, have children, and look back on this stage of their life with fondness.

Walking down the boardwalk of the main street, she nodded to the shopkeepers opening their stores and the early risers who had ventured out to shop before the weather became unbearable.

That was the one thing about working at the Silver Dollar Saloon, Beau had made it clear to everyone in the town, his girls did not fraternize with the men who came to the saloon. They delivered drinks, sang, and danced. None of the men who came through the door were allowed to touch the girls or even speak ill of them. Because of this, his saloon girls were treated with more respect around town than the ones in saloons where the women were told to allow the men to pull them onto their laps and go upstairs to give the men favors.

She shuddered thinking how she'd never be able to stand life if she were told she had to do favors for a man she didn't even know. Criminy, she'd known the three young men who'd attacked her, and she'd hated every second of their hands on her and their forced entry of her body. She would rather die than have any part of a man touching her that way.

Shoving those thoughts away, she stepped into the mercantile. Mr. Flanagan stood behind the counter reading a ledger.

He glanced up. "Miss Lottie Mae, what can I help you with?"

"I'd like a slate, chalk, eraser, pad, pencil, and a first reader, please." She slid the silver dollar across the counter.

"This sounds like you are teaching. I didn't realize you were qualified." Mr. Flanagan walked away from the counter to retrieve the items she'd requested.

Because he'd left, she took that as a good reason to ignore his comment. She would love to tell everyone in town she was indeed a school teacher and not a saloon girl, but that would also mean telling them the reason she no longer taught. She couldn't stomach telling anyone outside the boarding house about that.

Mr. Flanagan returned with the items, wrapping them in brown paper and tying twine around the bundle.

He counted back her change. "You helping one of the other ladies at the boarding house learn to read?"

She'd already made sure every woman in the boarding house could read and write. Having an education was one way Beau made sure they would be ready for a husband and family and it made them feel good about themselves.

"No. I'm helping Mr. Albrecht. He wishes to be able to read and write English." She figured people were going to find out sooner or later if she kept showing up at his blacksmith shop in the mornings.

"You do good by him and I'm sure there are others around here who would like to learn, too. Good day."

"Good day," she replied, thinking about what the mercantile owner had said. She wouldn't mind helping people one on one to learn English. There were a lot of people around here that spoke another language much better than they did the language of the country where they now lived.

Outside, she turned toward the train depot and stepped into the street. Dust poofed up around her skirt as she walked. The hot August days were baking the dirt and making it as powdery as flour. She stepped onto the board walkway and shook out her skirts. To her right was the side of the Allman Hotel. She walked along the brick building until she came to the city park. The open lot was the crowning glory of the town with shade trees and green grass that was watered by Clyde Dewerst, the town lamplighter and park attendant.

The large leafy trees gave a bit of relief from the summer sun. She walked through the park enjoying the shade and cool grass. After angling through the oasis, she looked up and spotted the blacksmith shop. Her belly started squiggling with nerves.

Manfred stepped out of the smaller door to the building. He spotted her and smiled.

He wore clean clothes, his face was shaved smooth, and his light brown hair was slicked back off his face. While she wouldn't say his face was handsome, it was memorable and fascinating. His brown eyes were lighter than most brown eyes she'd seen. His jaw square, rugged. His nose the right size for his face but the end curved slightly to the right. It was the lack of anger on his face that left it sleek, without the creases she'd witnessed on so many other men who went through life angry and fretful.

"Miss Lottie, you are early. I had wished to catch you in the park. We could sit on the bench under the trees where it is not so hot." He waved a hand toward the park.

"That is a lovely idea. I cut through there on my way here to enjoy the shade." She waited for him to come abreast of her, and they walked back to the park side by side.

"What have you brought?" he asked, when she was seated on the bench and he had sat on the ground beside the bench.

"I purchased items you will need to help you learn."

"You should not spend money on me. I can repay you." He shoved a hand into his trouser pocket.

"No. It is the way I prefer to teach. You don't need to pay for the items." She put a hand on his arm. It felt as big around as her leg. Heat shot up her arm and settled in her chest.

He glanced down at where her hand still rested.

She pulled it back and busied her fingers with untying the twine on the bundle. Her fingers fumbled, and he took the package from her.

Manfred broke the string as if it were a cobweb.

Her heart fluttered.

He picked up each item, inspecting them. "These are all things I remember from my childhood."

"I'm afraid to teach you English, we'll have to start as if you are that young boy again."

He grinned mischievously. "But there is no little girl with pigtails for me to pull."

Lottie Mae could see that this large man would have been the big boy in the class and he would have enjoyed tormenting the others. Not in a bad way but as a way to take their attention off his size.

"No little girls in this class." She peered into his eyes and her breath caught. The interest in the depth of his eyes sent her mind spinning.

"Let's start with the alphabet." She held out her hand. "Slate and chalk, please."

He handed her the items and sat crossed-legged, his attention on her hand as she wrote and recited the alphabet. "Now repeat after me."

Manfred repeated what Lottie said and understood these letters had different sounds than he grew up learning. But even better than understanding the letters, was watching and listening to Lottie. Her copper hair glistened under a strip of sunlight slipping through the tree's shade. Her creamy oval face and dark brown eyes with flecks of copper glanced from him to the slate and back to him as she waited for him to repeat the letters.

Her rosy pink lips were full, soft looking. It had been a long time since he'd fantasized about the softness of a woman's lips.

He dropped his gaze and quickly raised it before she caught him admiring her full bosom and generous curves. She wasn't a slip of a woman. Lottie would be a heavenly armful of soft woman.

The blood coursing through his body hit his *schwanz* at the same time he realized he wasn't repeating the letters.

"Manfred? Are you feeling alright? You look like you're overly heated."

The concern in her voice and worry on her face started his heart hammering in his chest. This wouldn't do. He'd learn nothing if he didn't keep his mind on the slate and not her.

"I am fine." He cleared his throat and repeated the letters as she had said them.

He managed to keep his mind on the lesson until a buckboard pulled up to his shop. "I must go. Mr. Dentz comes a long way to get my help." He stood.

"Will this happen every morning?" Her brow furrowed.

"Ja. I cannot tell people I am busy. They wish to have work done by me." Manfred stood. "I must go. I will come to the saloon tonight, and we can discuss how to find time to teach me."

She nodded and gathered her things.

Manfred glanced over at Mr. Dentz walking into his shop. "I must go. Thank you." He strode out of the park and up to his shop as Mr. Dentz stepped out the door.

They greeted each other in German and continued

their conversation in their native language.

"Were you enjoying the shade of the park?" Mr. Dentz asked.

"Yes, that and I am learning English with Miss Lottie." Part of his decision to meet Lottie in the park was so anyone passing by would see they were teacher and student. He didn't want Lottie to be linked with any vicious rumors.

"Ah, it's a good idea to learn our new country's language and be able to communicate. Good for you." He put a hand on the side of his wagon. "My mower broke. Can you fix it?"

Manfred looked into the back of the wagon. He could forge a new piece. "I can. You must leave it and I will get started." He walked to the back of the wagon and pulled on the mower. It was heavy, but not more than he could drag into the building.

"Don't hurt yourself," Mr. Dentz said, stepping up to help him.

"Stand back. I'll pull it out and drag it inside." Manfred tugged on the machinery. It dropped to the ground, jolting his arm sockets. Mr. Dentz helped him drag it into the building.

"Thank you," he said, straightening and wiping the sweat from his brow.

"You're welcome. If this is ready on Sunday may I pick it up after church?" Mr. Dentz asked.

"Yes." He took Sunday off. A thought came to him. After he loaded the mower, he could spend several hours learning with Lottie.

Chapter Four

Lottie Mae went back to the boarding house, a bit bewildered. Manfred wanted to learn, yet, they had barely started, and he'd hopped up to get back to work. She understood he had to work to live. Yet, it had been his idea to learn.

"Where have you been?" Belle asked, stepping out of the parlor with a duster in her hand. Her curly brown hair was hidden beneath a head covering of muslin.

"I was teaching Manfred, but he left as soon as Mr. Dentz arrived." She pulled her bonnet off her head. "I can't teach him if he leaves in the middle of a lesson."

Belle flicked the feather duster at the edge of the doorway. "Then you'll have to find a time to work with him when he won't be distracted."

Seeing her friend wielding a duster reminded Lottie Mae that she was going to suggest Beau have Dallie work at the boarding house two or three days a week.

"I'll be right back." She placed the school items on the stairs and marched down the hall.

Freedom and Liesa were in the kitchen, ironing.

Liesa glanced at Lottie Mae. Her porcelain skin was dotted with perspiration.

"You should sprinkle some of that water on yourself," Lottie Mae said.

"We're thinking about a cool dip in the bathing tub when we finish," Freedom picked up one of the three irons heating on the back of the cook stove.

"That would be refreshing." Lottie Mae noticed the fresh cookies on a plate. She put six of them on a small plate. "I'm going to talk with Beau about Dallie coming to help out a few days a week."

"That's a good idea. I don't mind doing this work, but by the end of the week, working in the saloon so many hours, I can barely keep my eyes open during Sunday Service." Freedom pressed down on the skirt, Liesa had sprinkled water on. The iron hissed and steam curled up around Freedom's hands and arms, glistening her face.

"I'll be back to help after I sweeten up Beau and ask him." Lottie Mae walked out the kitchen door, across the alley, and into the back of the saloon.

Beau was in the store room counting bottles of whiskey.

"Could you use a break?" she asked, walking up to him, holding the plate of cookies.

He glanced at the cookies and raised his gaze to her. "What do you want?"

She smiled. He sounded gruff, but they'd all

learned that was just his way. Underneath that gruffness was a soft, caring heart. She'd never known another man who would do as much as he did for women he didn't know and not expect a thing from them in return.

"Can we sit down?" she suggested.

He nodded and walked out to the bar. There were half a dozen men sitting at two tables. They were the mid-day locals who came in to talk about the railroad, the crops, and government.

Beau sat at the table closest to the back room.

Jules must have seen the cookies. He appeared at the table and plucked two from the plate. He stood, nibbling on a cookie and watching them.

Beau finally picked up a cookie. After swallowing a bite, he said, "Why did you bring cookies in here to bribe me?"

Lottie Mae smiled at him and then Jules. "I was talking to Dallie the other day. She loves being married, but she has a lot of time on her hands. I saw how tired Mrs. Dearling was at eight this morning. She can't keep doing everything at the boarding house. We help out as much as we can, but we're tired from working here and then trying to help. Why don't you hire Dallie to help Mrs. Dearling two or three days a week? She could do the laundry and the cleaning. The harder jobs in the house." She studied Beau. He was a hard person to discern what he was thinking.

"I'll have a visit with Dallie. If she does need something to do, I'll ask her to help out Mrs. Dearling." He held up a hand. "But we'll have to tell Mrs. Dearling that Dallie asked to come back to work because she was bored."

She stood and kissed Beau's cheek. "You're a good

man, Mr. Gentry."

The men took the last two cookies, and she picked up the plate. Life at the boarding house would get easier for everyone again. When Dallie stayed with them, she had taken up a lot of the load she, Belle, Freedom, and Liesa had been trying to do.

Back at the boarding house, she quietly told everyone that her plan had been a success. No one wanted to hurt Mrs. Dearling's feelings.

At two o'clock, they all dressed to go to work, sat down for a light meal, and headed over to the saloon. Lottie Mae was surprised to see Reverend Webster at the bar. Since marrying Savannah, Beau's sister, Lark rarely came to the saloon anymore.

Beau and Lark were deep in conversation at the end of the bar closest to the door. She sauntered over to Jules. "What are they discussing?"

He shook his head. "Don't know. Lark came in here looking pretty upset."

Beau glanced their direction. "Lottie Mae."

She hurried over to him. "Yes?"

"Lark says Savannah has a young woman over at the church who needs medical attention and a place to stay. She's adamant she wants to die in the church."

Lottie Mae sucked in her breath. "Is she going to die?" She peered at Lark.

He shook his head. "No. She was attacked on the train and dumped off the back onto the tracks."

"Then someone will come looking for her?" The word attacked started shivers up her back. She knew how the girl felt. From the knowing look in Beau's eyes, he knew that.

"I'll change out of this and go see if I can help Savannah." Lottie Mae hurried back through the supply room and across the alley to the house.

"What's the hurry?" Mrs. Dearling asked, turning from the sink where she washed dishes.

"Savannah has a hurt young woman at the church. I'm going to go help her." She walked over and gave Mrs. Dearling a hug. It was for her own sake that she held onto the stalwart woman. "We'll take her to the doctor and then she's going to need a room."

Mrs. Dearling hugged her and stepped back. "I'll get the room next to yours ready."

That's what she loved about this house and the people who were connected to it. They helped unconditionally.

She ran up the stairs, threw off her saloon dress, and donned her green skirt and calico bodice. Unsure what condition the woman's clothes would be in, she grabbed one of her everyday dresses, underclothes, stockings and shoes. She knew from experience; the woman would want to rid herself of any scent or reminder of what had happened. She would also want a hot bath.

Dr. Nolan lived across the street from the boarding house. Lottie strode across the street and knocked on his door.

"Coming!" he called out as heavy footsteps grew louder.

The door opened. "Miss Lottie Mae, what can I do for you?" His gaze fell on the dress hanging from her arm.

"Reverend Webster came to the saloon asking for help with a young woman who refuses to leave the church. She's been hurt." She dropped her gaze unsure what more to say.

"I'll get my bag and meet you there."

"No. Don't come to the church. Savannah and I will bring her to Savannah's house. She'll want to clean up and…" Lottie Mae swallowed. She didn't want the doctor knowing she had experience with the feelings this woman would have. "Just wait for us in the Webster house."

She swung around and practically ran to the church three blocks down the street. Lark stood outside the building when she arrived.

"Take a breath. There's no hurry, she's not going anywhere," he said.

"How much did she tell you?" Lottie Mae shifted the clothing to her other arm.

"Me. Nothing. I listened as Savannah managed to get a little out of her." He let out a sigh. "That woman I married surprises me every day."

Lottie Mae smiled. "You two are a good couple." She shoved the church door open and scanned the inside.

Savannah sat in a pew near the front of the church. She shifted her head slightly to acknowledge Lottie Mae.

Walking slowly, Lottie Mae made her way to the front of the church. A woman with blonde hair who looked no bigger than a young girl knelt in front of the altar. Her clothing was dirty and torn. The soles of her shoes were worn through to her stockings in spots.

"Darie? A friend of mine has brought you clean clothes," Savannah said.

"I do not want clean clothes. I want God to take me from this earth." The pain in her voice tore at Lottie Mae's heart.

"Darie?" Lottie Mae draped the clothing over the back of a pew and knelt beside the woman, not touching her. "Darie, don't give the pig who did this to you the satisfaction of winning."

The woman turned sky blue eyes on her. "He was filthier than a pig." Anger and humiliation shone in the woman's eyes.

"Be stronger, braver than the coward who did this to you. Only a coward would hurt a woman because he is too little of a man to fight another man." These were all things she'd said to herself when her family and the community shunned her.

"You can go on. I know you can." Lottie Mae waited for the woman to look at her again. When she did, she said, "I know because it happened to me five years ago."

The woman shook her head, but her gaze remained locked on Lottie Mae.

"Yes. Three young men waited for me to leave the school house." She stopped and swallowed. "And they… All three of them."

Tears ran down her cheeks and Darie's. They fell into each other's arms and embraced.

"I can help you. Savannah and Reverend Webster, Dr. Nolan, and the women I live with at the boarding house can all help you." Lottie Mae leaned back. "We can help, but I'll be the first to tell you some days aren't easy. But they are easier with friends like I have at the boarding house."

The woman didn't look completely convinced.

"I know what you want. A nice hot bath and I brought you clothes, but I'm afraid my clothes will be way to large on you." She glanced over at Savannah. "Once we get you in a bath, Savannah could go to the boarding house and get a set of clothes from Liesa. She's more your size."

Savannah nodded.

"How about it? Ready to go into Savannah's house right next door and take a bath? Dr. Nolan will be there, too. You look like you could use some bandages." Lottie Mae eased to her feet and held out her hand to help the other woman up.

Darie's left arm hung at her side and she winced.

Lottie Mae put an arm around the woman's shoulders. "Savannah, why don't you tell that husband of yours to take a walk for a while."

Savannah smiled and hurried down the aisle ahead of them.

"Another thing I know. You won't want men looking at you for a while. I know I didn't. It feels like everyone who looks at you knows what happened. But they don't. No one in this town will know unless you want them to." Lottie walked her out of the church and across the span of grass to Savannah and Lark's house. "Everyone who lives at the boarding house has been wronged terribly by a man. We all have stories we'll share with you. Private stories that are only to help you understand you are not alone."

The woman nodded slightly.

Lottie Mae opened the door to the Webster's house and walked them both inside.

Dr. Nolan sat in a chair at the kitchen table.

Darie stopped.

"This is Dr. Nolan. He is one of the friends I told you about who won't tell anyone what happened. You can trust him." Lottie Mae eased the woman over to the doctor. "Dr. Nolan, this is Darie."

Lottie Mae sat the woman on a chair. "Don't worry. I'm not leaving you." She stood beside the chair, her stomach churning, knowing how the woman felt.

"Darie, how did this happen?" Dr. Nolan asked.

The woman shook her head.

"Don't worry about how it happened, Dr. Nolan, just check to see how badly she's hurt," Lottie Mae said.

Gratitude shone in Darie's eyes.

The doctor nodded his head and started at Darie's head, checking all the places that were bloody or scratched. At her left arm, he shook his head. "You dislocated your shoulder."

He glanced at Lottie Mae. "She needs to expose her arm and shoulder. That way I can see to put the arm back in the socket."

Lottie Mae looked into Darie's eyes. "The only way to fix your arm is to drop your bodice to your waist."

Fear sparked in the woman's eyes.

"I'll be right here. The only thing the doctor will touch is your arm and shoulder. I'll help you put the bodice down."

Darie's lips trembled but she nodded once.

With nimble fingers, Lottie Mae unbuttoned the bodice of Darie's dress and helped her ease the injured arm out of the sleeve.

Dr. Nolan explained what he would do before he

slowly took hold of Darie's arm with one hand and her shoulder with the other.

She cried out when he jerked her arm.

But when he removed his hands, her left arm didn't hang limply at her side.

Tears trickled down the woman's face.

"Darie, do you have any other injuries that I can't see?" Dr. Nolan asked.

She shook her head.

"Then I'll leave you to get cleaned up." The doctor stood, picked up his bag, and headed to the door.

"Dr. Nolan, Beau will pay the bill." Lottie Mae said.

He nodded and closed the door behind him.

"I'll get the stove stoked, and you can get a hot bath." Lottie walked over to the door of the bathing room. "If you want to go in there and take off your clothes and start the cold water running into the tub, I'll bring in the hot water from the reservoir on the stove."

Darie sat in the chair. "Why are you helping me? I am no good now."

"Don't say that. You are the same person you were before this happened. Only stronger. To survive what you and I went through and go on, it makes us tough."

"No man will want a woman who-who—"

"You're wrong. Beau Gentry, Savanah's brother, owns the Silver Dollar Saloon. He has taken in nearly a dozen women like you and me. We live in the boarding house with Mrs. Dearling and work in the saloon until we find husbands, marry, and have the same life as any other woman." She walked over and helped Darie to her feet, leading her to the bathing room. "Right now, it's hard to imagine. But in a year or two, you'll feel differently. Go in and start the water."

Darie stopped. "Why do you all do so much for a stranger?"

"We were all strangers once."

Chapter Five

Lottie Mae hauled a bucket of hot water to the bathing room. She opened the door and discovered Darie sitting on a chair still in her underclothes, staring at the cold water that rushed into the tub from the faucet. Lottie Mae turned off the water before they would have to pull the plug to make room for the hot water she'd brought.

"What's wrong Darie?" she asked.

The young woman sat with her arms crossed, hugging her body and shivering.

"Don't worry this hot water I brought in will warm up your bath," Lottie Mae said, pouring the steaming water into the tub.

The girl shook her head.

Lottie Mae looked down, catching sight of the blood on the hemline of Darie's shift "Come on get in the tub. You'll feel better just getting out of those clothes." With much coaxing, she managed to get Darie to stand and allow her to draw the shift up over her head. The young woman's body had scrapes and bruises. Purple markings in the shape of fingers stood out against the woman's pale skin on her hips.

Anger bubbled in Lottie Mae. If the person who had done this to Darie was standing in front of her, she could easily have put a bullet through his heart. Why were men so cruel?

"Step on in the water. It'll make you feel better." She helped Darie step over the edge of the tub and slowly lower into the water. When the young woman was settled, Lottie Mae handed her a rag and sweet-smelling soap she'd brought from her room. She knew that the best way to help the young woman forget about her experience was to get rid of the smell and feel clean.

"Scrub away all that dirt and all that blood and we'll have a look at you to make sure everything is okay." Lottie Mae stood with her hand on the door. "I'll leave and give you some privacy. I'll be just outside the door. Give a holler if you need anything, otherwise I'll be back shortly"

Lottie Mae stepped out of the room. Her whole body shook. She'd remained strong while helping Darie. Seeing the bruises, the willingness to die, and the belief no one would care for her now, brought back all the memories of her humiliation at the hands of three young men. Even though she'd pulled through and realized it wasn't her fault, the old fears and humiliation crept into her mind.

How could anyone treat another person the way that someone had treated them? The young woman had bruises all over her body. Part were from being thrown off the train. Others were made by the man's cruelty. The worst scars would be the deeper emotional scars. Lottie Mae knew they would last a lot longer than the bruises.

"How is that poor little girl doin'?" asked Savannah.

"About as good as could be expected. That young thing has been through a lot in the last day or so. I hope they find the man who did that to her." Lottie Mae wanted to charge down the street and find Sheriff Blake. He should be told about the assault upon Darie. But it wasn't her place to do that. She had to talk Darie into doing it herself.

"Do you think she'll have the gumption to tell the sheriff what happened?" Savannah asked.

"I don't know. She's scared. And I know from my experience, it's hard to get past the humiliation that this happened to you. I'm a big woman. When you think what that poor little thing felt like with some man attacking her." Anger bubbled in her chest at not just the man who'd hurt Darie but all men. It was a hate that she was still working on. It didn't include Beau or Jules. They had proved many times over, the way they protected everyone in the boarding house, that they didn't condone the mistreatment of women.

Savannah shook her head, sympathy in her eyes. "I can't even imagine what y'all went through. What is wrong with a man that would harm a woman in such a way?"

"I don't know. But I wish we could string him up and cut off his parts."

Lottie Mae waited ten minutes before she knocked on the door and entered. When she opened the door, Darie sat in the cold water, her arms wrapped around herself again. Lottie Mae walked in, stealing her gaze away from all the bruises and scratches that could be seen above the water.

"Are you clean now?" she asked.

Darie just stared down at the water.

Lottie Mae walked over with the large towel that Savannah had handed her to give to the young woman. "Here you go, step on out. We'll get you dried off and some new clothes on. That will make you feel a whole lot better."

She held up the towel, concealing her view of the young woman stepping out of the tub. When she felt the woman pushing against the towel, Lottie Mae wrapped the cloth around Darie.

"Let me drain this water and I'll help you dress." It took a strong constitution to put her hand in the vermillion colored water and pull the plug. A lot of blood had tinted the water. She didn't think all the blood had been on the young woman.

Shifting her gaze to Darie, she noticed rivulets of blood trickling down her legs.

Lottie Mae went to the door and opened it only wide enough to poke her head out. "Savannah, could you be so kind as to bring me monthly rags?"

The woman's mouth opened, but she didn't say a word and scurried out of the kitchen.

Lottie Mae knew the young woman should be checked by the doctor, but she doubted Darie would allow it. She'd been violated in the most invasive way and wouldn't care to have someone inspecting the damage.

Shutting the door, she found Darie in front of the small mirror on the wall, staring.

"I know you feel like your body has been taken from you and you'll never be the same. But I can tell you from experience, you have to give yourself time. Don't dwell on what happened. It will only make you crazy. You are with people who understand and will help you. It took me finding Beau and the women who live here, and time. I'm finally feeling like I can love a man. That I can stand the touch of a man other than Beau and Jules. It will take time, but you will, too." Lottie rubbed the towel on Darie's body.

The young woman winced and cried out.

"I'm sorry. I forgot." She released the towel. "I'll let you dry yourself." Lottie turned her back to the young woman.

A soft knock on the door gave her something to do.

Savannah handed her the cotton rags and ties she used to hold them on. "Is she…harmed?"

Lottie Mae gave a slight nod and took the cloth, closing the door.

"You'll want to wear this for a day or so." Lottie handed the cloth to Darie.

The young woman stared at it a moment, before tucking it between her legs with a grimace.

"We can call Dr. Nolan to come back and take a look at you down there."

The young woman's eyes widened in fright.

"I wouldn't leave you alone with him, and he'd be gentle." Lottie Mae didn't want the woman to think she was trying to bring her more torture.

"No. I don't want anyone…" Darie hiccupped and wiped at the tears trickling down her cheeks.

"Then I won't contact him." As she helped the woman dress, she said, "Did you know the man who attacked you?"

Darie froze and her body started to shudder.

"There, I didn't mean to cause you fright. It's just if he happens to come around, Beau needs to know to keep him away from you and the other women he could hurt."

Darie peered into her eyes. "You think he's done this to more than me?"

She shrugged. "What he did to you was that of a monster. I wouldn't doubt he has done it to others."

For the first time, the woman seemed to be thinking of something other than her attack. "He pretended to like me when we first met on the train." Her cheeks darkened. "He was handsome, spoke well, and appeared to truly care about my comfort."

"Where did you get on the train?" Lottie helped her into the drawers and shift.

"A small town outside of Minneapolis. I was headed to my first teaching job in Montana." She shook her head. "I can't go there now. I couldn't…couldn't help the children feeling like I do now." Tears began again.

"Shhh. Beau will send a telegraph saying you've been detained." She picked up a dress Savannah had borrowed from Liesa's room. She was the only one close to Darie's size. "Tell me about this man. Did he tell you his name?" Lottie May held the dress up for Darie to duck under.

"He said his name was Thomas."

Lottie's hands shook. One of the young men who had attacked her five years ago was named Thomas. Thomas Decker. He had been good looking with curly blond hair. She settled the dress over Darie's head and peered into her eyes. "What did he look like?"

"His hair was blond and curly. His eyes were dark blue almost black. There was a crook in his nose, like he'd broken it." Darie shuddered. "I thought he was nice until he walked me to the baggage car and…" Her hands fisted and her face lost color.

"Forget I asked." Lottie Mae picked up a brush and drew it through Darie's hair. Once her hair was brushed and braided, Lottie Mae opened the door and walked her to the boarding house.

Chapter Six

Freedom and Mrs. Dearling sat at the kitchen table talking softly when Lottie Mae ushered Darie into the boarding house. She motioned for the young woman to sit on one of the benches. "Freedom and Mrs. Dearling, I'd like to introduce you to Darie. She'll be staying with us for a while."

Freedom smiled and held out her hand. "Welcome Darie, I'm sure you'll have a nice stay with us."

Mrs. Dearling reached across the table and patted Darie's hand. "You're a welcome addition to the household."

"I think Darie would like something to eat," Lottie Mae said.

Mrs. Dearling stood and scurried over to the stove, humming and stirring a pot.

Freedom glanced from Lottie Mae to Darie and

back to Lottie Mae. "Are you going to be able to work tonight?"

"We'll see how things go here. I don't want to leave Darie alone right now." Lottie Mae placed her hand on the young woman's shoulder.

Darie shied away from the touch.

Lottie Mae removed her hand and shook her head.

Freedom stood and walked towards the door. "I'll let Beau know." She left through the back door.

Mrs. Dearling placed a bowl of soup in front of Darie. "Here you go, Dearie. This will warm your insides."

Lottie Mae knew that food wouldn't help the emptiness that the young woman felt. However, food is what Mrs. Dearling thought solved everything. If it made the older woman feel as if she was contributing to the younger woman's care, that was all that mattered.

Darie didn't pick up a spoon or even sniff the soup.

Lottie Mae sat down beside the young woman, her hands in her lap, letting her know she wasn't alone. There was nothing she could do at this moment to make Darie feel any different than she did. But she could give strength through just being close at hand.

After fifteen minutes and the young woman still hadn't eaten her soup, Lottie Mae decided she needed to do something.

"Why don't you go upstairs and lie down for a while, Darie. I think the rest will do you good," Lottie Mae said.

Darie stood, appearing relieved to be allowed to hide away in a room.

"Come along. I'll show you to your room," said

Lottie Mae. She led the young woman down the hall and up the stairs. "Your room is the one right next to mine. If you need me during the night, all you have to do is come to my room." She showed the young woman which door was hers and then walked to the one down the hallway and opened it. "This will be your room for as long as you want to stay here."

"Why is everyone being nice to me? You don't know me." Darie peered at her. Her fear had been replaced with suspicion.

Lottie Mae smiled down at the young woman. "Because this house and the man who owns it, have been saving women like us for years. Beau Gentry is a man with integrity and one you can trust with your life. He's saved all of ours. Freedom's, Liesa's, Belle's, mine, Mrs. Dearling's and many more before us and will surely be after us."

Darie studied her for several seconds and asked, "Who is Beau Gentry?"

"You'll meet him when the time is right." Lottie Mae led her into the room. It was like hers and all the other bedrooms in the house. A nice sized bed with a pretty quilt made by Mrs. Dearling. Lacy curtains on the window. One wardrobe to hold their clothes. A washstand with porcelain pitcher and bowl and a chamber pot on the bottom. It was the nicest room Lottie Mae had ever stayed in. She knew it was the same for most of the other women that had been through this house.

"Get some sleep. When you feel up to it, wander down to the kitchen and Mrs. Dearling and I will be there." She left the young woman sitting on the bed as she stepped out of the room and closed the door.

Lottie Mae knew that the first days and weeks would be the hardest for the young girl. She would be there just as Beau, Mrs. Dearling, and the other women in the house had helped her when Beau had picked her up alongside the road nearly starved and fighting off anyone who came near her.

She descended the stairs thinking about Darie and wondering when she would be able to go back to the saloon. As much as she didn't care for working there, it was something to do. She liked to be busy. It kept her mind from wandering to things that only made her sad.

Down in the kitchen, Mrs. Dearling started asking questions Lottie Mae couldn't answer. Because they weren't her answers to give.

"But when do you think she'll be ready to go out?" Mrs. Dearling asked.

"I don't know. She's in shock at the moment. And she may not want to be around any males for quite some time." Lottie Mae knew that Beau would be able to gain Darie's trust before any other man. Just like he'd calmly talked her into climbing into his wagon. She'd instinctively known he wouldn't hurt her. His soft tone, caring eyes, and the way he never made a move to touch her had given her the courage to trust in him.

"What about church on Sunday? Surely, the poor dear will want to pray for guidance." Mrs. Dearling placed a cup of tea on the table in front of Lottie Mae.

The mention of church had her thinking about Sunday and how Manfred never worked on Sunday. Perhaps, that was the day they could work on his schooling. "I can't sit around here all day waiting to see if Darie needs me."

Mrs. Dearling glanced at her. "Do you plan to go to the saloon?"

"Yes. You can come get me if she needs me." Lottie Mae hurried out into the hall and up the stairs to change into her saloon dress.

Lottie Mae looked in on Darie before she headed over to the saloon. The young woman was sleeping soundly.

When she arrived in the saloon, Beau pulled her to the side and asked how the woman was doing.

"She'll need time," Lottie Mae said.

Beau got the look in his eyes that he had every time he found a woman that had been brutalized by a man. He slammed his fist on the bar, causing all the patrons to turn around and look.

She put a hand on his arm. "Don't lose your temper. You can't show any anger when you meet her. She's going to be scared of men for a while. Much worse than I was." She couldn't shut down the emotions and memories of that night. They returned when she least expected them.

Beau studied her. "Is this bringing back too many memories for you?"

"They've been haunting me a lot more lately. But seeing her, seeing her bruises, her tears and fear, it brings that night back clearly in my mind." She didn't want to talk about it even with Beau. She picked up a tray and headed out among the tables to take drink orders. Even though she hated doing this part of the job, she knew that she owed the man standing behind the bar her whole life.

She'd been in the saloon an hour when Mrs.

Dearling charged in from the back room. "Lottie Mae! Lottie Mae, you need to come! That young thing's havin' a fit up there."

Lottie Mae dropped the tray she was carrying onto the bar and headed through the back room, across the alley, and up the stairs to Darie's bedroom.

The young woman was screaming and flailing around in the quilts on the bed.

"It's okay. I'm here. No one's going to hurt you," Lottie Mae said as she untangled the woman from the bedding and calmed her down.

"Get away! Get away!" Darie screamed.

"I won't hurt you. It's me, Lottie Mae," she said, trying to bring the young woman out of her nightmare.

The young woman sat up in bed and sobbed. Lottie Mae held her close. "You're going to be all right." She ran a hand down Darie's soft blonde hair. "You're going to be fine. No one's going to hurt you here." Lottie Mae continued to hold the girl until her sobs subsided.

"I know right now this feels like you're never gonna get over what happened. But you will, I promise." Lottie Mae held the young woman away from her. Her eyes were wide and wild. Her lips quivered.

"No one is going to hurt you here. Look at me." She held onto Darie's shoulders until she finally peered into her eyes. "You are safe here. No one will hurt you. Why don't you go down and help Mrs. Dearling in the kitchen? Being busy will help chase the fears away."

Darie sniffed and wiped a hand under her nose. She thought for a minute and slowly nodded her head.

Lottie Mae helped the young woman to her feet.

"Why are you dressed like that?" Darie asked.

"Because I was working at the Silver Dollar Saloon. Beau Gentry, our benefactor, owns the saloon and gives us a job there until we find other jobs or marry." Many times, Lottie Mae had to defend why she worked in the saloon. But she'd never once felt as if what she did was wrong. What had been done to her that caused her to work in a saloon was more wrong than delivering drinks to men and dancing.

"How can you… you walk around dressed like that in a room full of men if you also were…were…" Darie's gaze flicked from her modest neckline that showed more neck and chest than the high collared dresses most women wore, to the skirt that stopped at her knees.

"Beau and his partner, Jules, won't let the men touch us when we're working. If anyone says something horrible to us, Beau and Jules throw the man out of the saloon. It's not like other saloons. Beau and Jules run a sophisticated place." Lottie Mae walked to the door and opened it. "Come on. Mrs. Dearling will enjoy your help."

Darie followed her down the stairs and into the kitchen. Mrs. Dearling turned from the counter where she was putting a tea pot on a tray.

"Darie would like to help you to take her mind off things." Lottie Mae said.

Darie stepped forward, nodding her head.

"Good for you child," said Mrs. Dearling. "I can use the help."

Lottie Mae left Darie helping the housekeeper in the kitchen and headed back across the alley and into the saloon.

When she reappeared, Beau came over to see what had happened.

"I have her working in the kitchen with Mrs. Dearling. It's best to keep her busy and not let her think about what has happened." Lottie Mae picked up the tray with fresh mugs of beer.

Beau put a hand on her arm, stopping her. "Do you think she'll be able to tell us who did it?"

Lottie Mae had gained the young woman's confidence. Telling Beau she knew the man was called Thomas and he had curly blond hair could have him pressing Darie for more information and have the young woman not confide in her anymore.

"Eventually, she probably will. Right now, she doesn't even want to think about it." Lottie Mae looked down at his hand on her arm. Beau released her, and she moved about the room, once again, passing out beer and taking money.

Lottie Mae and Freedom went to the boarding house for their dinner. They entered the kitchen and found Darie helping set the table and put out the food. The young woman looked more at ease than she had when Lottie Mae left her. She smiled at Darie and sat in her spot at the table.

Freedom sat down at her spot and thanked both Darie and Mrs. Dearling for the food that was placed in front of her. They both began eating.

Darie sat down at the table along with them and nibbled on a piece of bread.

"Darie is a very good helper," Mrs. Dearling said.

"That's good. You could use the help." Freedom

waved her piece of bread around and smiled at Mrs. Dearling.

Lottie Mae wondered if Darie might work out to be the person to help take some of the workload off Mrs. Dearling instead of Dallie. She'd have to mention to Beau to wait to talk to Dallie about helping at the boarding house. From her own experience, she knew it was going to take months before Darie would be ready to work in the saloon.

When they finished eating, Lottie Mae and Freedom headed back to the saloon. They passed Liesa and Belle headed to the house for their dinner.

Lottie Mae was working behind the bar when Manfred entered the saloon.

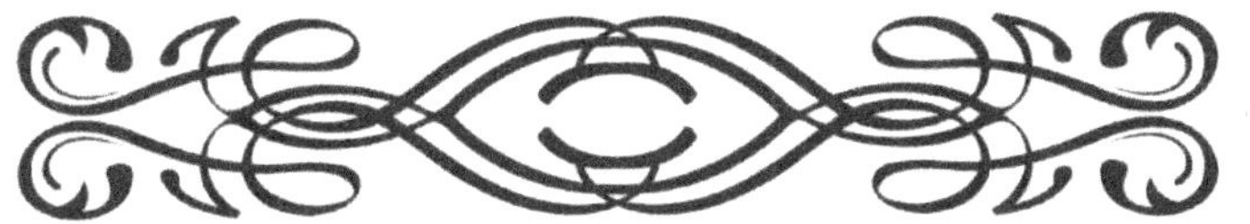

Chapter Seven

Manfred had spent half an hour trying to decide whether he should clean up before he went to the bar to see Lottie. He knew if he cleaned up others would take notice and while he wouldn't mind Miss Lottie knowing he'd cleaned up for her, he didn't really want everyone else to know. He'd decided to go as he was.

Standing inside the door, once again, unsure whether to go to the bar where Lottie Mae was working or go to a table, he found himself being pushed farther into the building by a couple of other patrons who walked through the door. He ended up deciding he'd rather not sit at a table with other people. The only place there was room left at the bar was near the end. He took up the same space he had the night before.

Beau worked his way down the bar and handed him a glass of beer.

"You seem to be spending a little more time in here

lately," Beau said.

Manfred's ears heated at the man's comment, as if he'd stayed too long next to his forge. "It's been warm out. Makes me thirsty." Manfred raised the mug of beer and swallowed several large gulps.

Beau smiled and walked to the other end, sending Miss Lottie down his direction. Just the sight of her started Manfred's heart beating in his chest like a hammer banging on a hunk of iron.

"Good evening, Manfred," Lottie said.

"Good evening, Miss Lottie." Manfred took another sip of his beer, but his eyes remained on Lottie, standing in front of him, smiling. Even her eyes lit up in welcome. Knowing that she gave him the full benefit of her smile, started his heart thumping all over again.

"Sorry I had to leave our lesson early. Mr. Dentz is a good customer. I did not want to have him think I did not want to do his work."

"I understand. But we're going to have to find the time for me to teach you when you aren't busy." She held up a finger and moved down the bar. Picking up an empty glass, she pivoted to the keg, filled the mug, and placed it back in front of the man. She plucked a coin from the counter in front of the man, put it in the till, and returned to him.

"I was thinking about that, too," he said. "We can do schooling Sunday afternoons. There would be more time." He studied her face to see if she liked the idea as much as he did.

Lottie Mae's eyes lit up, and she smiled even bigger. "I was thinking the same thing."

Manfred's smile had to be spread clear across his face. Seeing her happiness, made his heart warm.

She continued filling shot glasses and mugs up and down the bar.

Manfred sipped his beer, watching Lottie smile and converse with the other customers. While she seemed comfortable visiting with the men, her gaze every so often went over to him and he'd see a genuine smile on her lips before she would go back to speaking with the others. He turned a little from the bar, studying the other girls as they worked. Even though he had been a bouncer in here several times while Beau and Jules were gone, he had never really taken the time to watch the women. His job had been to make sure the men kept their hands to themselves and didn't say anything rude.

Tonight, he watched the women and noticed that they all, even though they smiled and carried on brief conversations with the men, never leaned toward them and their smiles never lit their eyes. Their stiff bodies, held away from the men, showed him they were uncomfortable.

Watching them made him wonder about their backgrounds and how they came to work in a saloon. He knew the women in this saloon were treated different than the women who worked in the other saloons in town. It was that difference that had him coming back to the Silver Dollar. He didn't care for the wanton rowdiness of the other saloons and how the women were treated. Here they were treated with respect.

Lottie worked her way down the bar toward him and stopped in front of him. "Would you like another mug of beer?"

Manfred smiled at her and held up the half-full

mug in his hand. "No, I am taking my time."

She smiled at him, wiped the counter with a rag, and headed back to the other end of the bar.

He wondered why she was keeping her distance. His thoughts went back to how Beau kept the saloon respectable and worked to make the community respect the women who worked here. While they were starting up a teacher student relationship, others may not understand. He finished off his beer, caught Lottie's attention, nodded to her, and left the building. Not ready to retire to his small accommodations in the back of his blacksmith shop, Manfred decided to go for a walk. He rounded the corner and found himself walking in front of Mrs. Dearling's boarding house.

Screams filled the air.

He looked all around and couldn't see anyone in the street.

The screams grew louder.

He realized they were coming from the boarding house. He took the four steps up the front porch in two strides, pulled open the screen door, and stood in the entry.

Another scream pierced the air. It came from upstairs.

He took the stairs two at a time and found Mrs. Dearling standing at a door with her hands over her ears, trying to talk to someone. Manfred hurried to the door and pulled Mrs. Dearling back to look in.

A tiny young woman sat on the bed, clutching the covers and screaming. Her eyes were wide, staring, and filled with fear.

He talked to her in German in a soft voice and walked towards the bed. Her face was scratched and bruised. He wondered what horrors she had been through to cause such screeching. He continued talking and moving towards her.

Her head swung around. Her gaze landed on him. Her mouth opened but no screeching came out. Instead, her feet began moving. She shoved herself up to the head of the bed, clutching the covers around her tightly. "Go away! Go away!" she said in a hoarse voice.

Manfred stopped in the middle of the room. Footsteps rang out on the stairs.

Chapter Eight

Lottie Mae burst into the bedroom. She'd heard the screams as she'd headed to the privy behind the saloon. She'd ran past Mrs. Dearling standing in the hallway and through the bedroom door.

Manfred stood in the middle of the room. Concern and confusion marred his usual jovial face. Darie stood up against the head of the bed, clutching her covers, her eyes widened, her mouth moving but no sound coming out.

Lottie Mae touched Manfred's arm. "You need to go. She's scared of men."

Manfred looked from Darie to Lottie Mae and back to Darie. "You sure it is men? She looks terrified."

"Please, Manfred. You need to leave. You don't know what she's been through. It was a man who put those bruises on her." Lottie Mae turned Manfred toward the door.

He slowly walked out but stopped in the doorway "You can't tell me what happened?"

Lottie Mae nodded and waited for him to get out of sight. She moved to the bed, talking quietly. "You're safe. No one will hurt you."

The young woman lowered her gaze to Lottie Mae. Her body stopped quaking. Her white knuckles, clutching the covers, gradually regained color.

Mrs. Dearling entered the room. "I didn't know what to do for her. I just didn't know what to do."

Lottie Mae nodded her head. "It's okay. I'm here. I'll help you. I know what to do." Lottie Mae sat beside Darie, not touching her.

"I'll go make some tea." Mrs. Dearling trotted across the room and out the door.

Lottie Mae talked quietly, telling Darie she wasn't alone and no one was going to hurt her again.

By the time Mrs. Dearling brought up the tea, Darie had stopped shaking and her eyes no longer looked as if she had a fever. She seemed to be embarrassed.

Lottie Mae poured the tea into the cups and handed one to Darie. "Here you go. This will make you feel better. What else will make you feel better is telling me or the sheriff everything you can about the man who did this to you."

Darie's eyes widened and her head started to shake.

Lottie Mae picked up her cup of tea, sat down on the chair next to the bed, and studied the woman. She sipped her tea for a few minutes, trying to decide how to start the conversation. "Darie, I know you were hurt badly. The bruises, scrapes, and violation."

The young woman's eyes flashed with hatred for a brief moment.

Lottie Mae was happy to see that fire. It would give Darie the strength she needed to get stronger.

"The best way to stop the bad dreams is to tell somebody and get it off your mind. Talking about it will also help you realize that it wasn't your fault."

Darie shook her head but opened her mouth, and said, "It is so terrible. I-I don't know how to speak of it. I didn't do anything."

"I know you didn't. The fault all belongs to the man who did this to you. If you were willing to describe him or give all of his name to Sheriff Blake, he can make sure the man doesn't hurt anyone else."

Darie shook her head. "He said he would kill me if I told anybody. I can't say any more."

"If we don't know who to watch for, we can't help you." Lottie Mae set her cup and saucer down and grasped Darie's free hand. "The only way Beau, Jules, the women who live in this house, and Sheriff Blake can keep you safe and make sure the man doesn't hurt you, is if you tell us who he is."

"If I stay in this house, he'll never see me."

"Darie you can't live in this house forever. You are going to want to walk out in the sunshine, see the flowers, and explore life. You're too young to stay inside."

"Mrs. Dearling said that I can help her with the housework. I am good at housework. I can do that and stay inside."

Lottie Mae released Darie's hand and picked up her teacup. "You can stay in the house and you can help with the housework. But you're going to have to go out into the town at some point either on an errand or to church with the rest of us."

"I won't go to church. There was no help when I prayed to him to take my life. I will stay here in the house. I will work hard. I will be good. Do not make me go out of the house."

Lottie Mae realized that it would be a while before Darie would be able to go out into the community. However, her helping Mrs. Dearling would be a good thing for both the young woman and the older lady. What they had to take care of were these nightmares, or no one would get any sleep.

"I won't push you right now to tell us who the man is. But for your safety, you should." She set her cup down on the tray as did Darie. Lottie Mae picked up the tray with the cups. "Can I leave you alone?"

Darie nodded slightly. "It was just the dream. I am safe."

"The dreams will come for some years, but eventually they aren't as strong, and they don't wake you with such a fright." Lottie Mae walked to the door and turned back to Darie. "Try to get some sleep. If you can't, there is a book on the bedside table you may read. I'll check on you again when I get done working at the saloon."

Lottie Mae walked downstairs and was surprised to see Manfred standing in the doorway of the parlor.

"Is the girl better?"

She studied the concern on Manfred's face. Her heart tumbled in her chest. She had never come across a man that showed his emotions so easily. She knew everything he was thinking and felt. "She had a bad dream. She'll be fine. It will just take time."

"What happened to her? I saw the bruises and scratches on her face, and the scream. The way she was screaming, she was terrified."

Lottie Mae walked into the parlor and set the tray with the empty cups on the table. She motioned for Manfred to sit on the settee. His large frame took up over half of the seating. But she didn't mind sitting close to him. He was one of the three men she trusted enough to touch and not fear he would think she was open to his advances. She sat down next to him. Her arm brushed his and her skirt swished against his pant leg. She peered into his concern face. "A man attacked her on the train and threw her off."

The anger that flashed across Manfred's face made her lean back a bit. She knew he would never hurt her. His anger was for the man that would hurt a woman.

"Why would a man do such a thing to a little bitty thing like her?" His hands fisted, opened, and clenched again. His face slowly lost the anger, and he peered into her eyes. "What can I do to help?"

This was what she had come to love about this man. Never once did he worry about himself, but always about others. Not even knowing the young woman's name, he was willing to help her. Her feelings for this man grew and grew with each moment she was with him. "If I can get her to tell me who it was, we will need to watch out for him. He threatened to kill her if she told anyone."

Manfred shot to his feet and paced three steps across and three steps back, mumbling.

Lottie Mae watched the big man. She couldn't

understand his native language, but she knew cursing when she heard it.

"When you discover this man, I will help bring him to the sheriff." Manfred stopped in front of where she sat and held out a hand to her.

She put her hand in his. He drew her to her feet.

"No man should ever hurt a woman." His gaze traveled over her face, stopping at her lips and moving up to her eyes. "I would never hurt anyone, and especially, I would never hurt you."

The warmth of his big hand encasing hers, sent heat up her arm and jolted her body with sensations she'd never experienced before. The way her body heated, and her heart raced, she knew this man had broken through the wall she'd built the day her body had been taken from her. Tonight, she was having a breakthrough. It was one that she hoped continued with this man.

"Manfred, I know you are a gentle soul. And I know you would never hurt me. But I do have a history that someday I wish to tell you."

Sorrow filled his eyes. He gave her hand a gentle squeeze. "I know. Watching you and the other ladies in the saloon, you all have had bad times with men. I can tell by the way you act." He gave her hand a little tug, drawing her one step closer to him. He peered down into her face. "Your secrets are safe with me. I care for you too much to allow anything to come between us."

His unconditional acceptance of her was expanding her heart, opening her mind, and giving her all of the emotions that she had dreamed she would one day be able to feel for a man.

"What are you doing in my parlor and without a chaperone?" asked Mrs. Dearling as she rushed into the room.

Manfred released her hand as if it had just caught on fire and spun around to the plump little lady standing in the doorway with her hands on her hips. "I am—I was just visiting with Miss Lottie. I must go now." He strode to the door. Mrs. Dearling stepped to the side, and Manfred was gone.

Lottie Mae started giggling. The way the big man had hustled out of the room when the little elderly lady had got after him had made a comical sight.

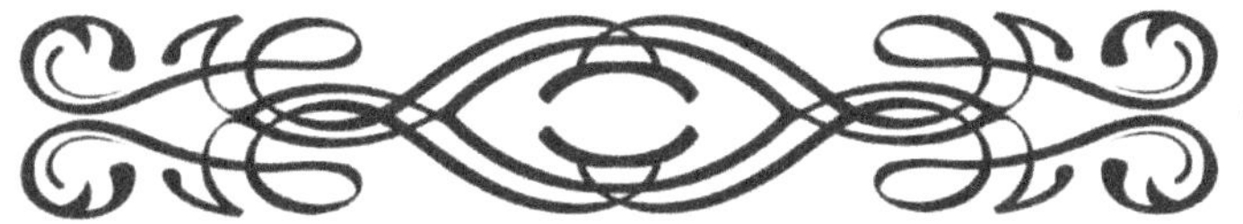

Chapter Nine

Lottie Mae had a hard time sitting still through Reverend Webster's sermon that Sunday. She had plans to meet Manfred in the park by his blacksmith shop right after church services. Ever since the evening when he had tried to help Darie, Lottie Mae had been finding the man on her thoughts more and more. His kind words and comment that he would be there for her and never hurt her sat nicely in her mind and kept her heart warm when a man at the saloon leered at her. The more she thought about being Mrs. Albrecht, she knew no man would dare say anything rude or to try anything with her. They would have to go through the mountain of a man that was Manfred Albrecht.

"My goodness, Lottie Mae, you are worse than that little boy three pews ahead of us," Belle said as she put a hand on Lottie Mae's leg, holding it from jittering.

Freedom leaned across Lottie Mae and said to Belle, "She's gonna give Manfred lessons after the sermon. She's in a hurry to get there." The two women giggled, causing the older women in the pew ahead of them to turn around and glare.

"Helping Manfred is good for me. I enjoy teaching," Lottie Mae whispered to her friend.

"And it helps that he has eyes for you," Freedom whispered back.

Lottie Mae shook her head at her friend, but she couldn't stop the grin that spread from ear to ear.

"And she likes him, too," Freedom said, pointing to Lottie Mae and looking at Belle.

"Shhh. You ladies need to be quiet," said Mrs. Dearling.

Lottie Mae folded her hands in her lap and stared forward, not hearing a word Reverend Webster said, waiting for the last prayer and Amen.

At the end of the sermon, Reverend Webster reminded everybody there would be a social at the end of the month and everyone was invited. He asked that the women of the congregation bring baked goods to be sold to raise money for more pews for the church.

Lottie Mae wondered if Manfred would attend the social. It would be wonderful to waltz in his arms. She'd surprised herself with that thought. It was the first time in five years she'd thought about dancing and merriment while in the presence of a man.

The congregation stood. Lottie Mae spotted Manfred in the back of the church. He was taller than anyone else, making it easy to spot his welcome face. His gaze scanned the room. The minute he caught hers, he smiled and nodded towards the door. She gave him a slight nod and followed the rest of the women out of the pew, into the aisle leading to the door, and outside. At the door she shook hands with Lark and Savannah and thanked Lark for such a wonderful sermon, even though she hadn't heard a word of it.

Lottie Mae followed the other women from the church to go back to the boarding house for the Sunday meal. Beau and Jules stood with Mrs. Dearling waiting for everyone to gather like a flock of chickens. As she walked over toward the group, Manfred walked up to Beau. Manfred and her boss had a short discussion. By the time Lottie Mae arrived at the group, all were smiling as Beau shook Manfred's hand.

Beau turned and looked at Lottie Mae. He smiled and motioned to Manfred. "I invited Manfred to our Sunday dinner, I hope you don't mind."

Disappointment lodged in Lottie Mae's throat. She had hoped to have Manfred all to herself. She didn't like having to pretend that the man meant nothing to her when she was with other people.

Her silence must have bothered Manfred, because he said, "I do not want to disturb your dinner I can—"

"No. No, having dinner with us is fine," Lottie Mae said, hoping to allay his fears that she didn't want him to have dinner with them.

Relief crossed Manfred's face and a smile bloomed.

Lottie Mae felt like a fool for having worried about not getting to spend time alone with Manfred. After they had dinner, they could go to the park and work on his English. There it would be the two of them.

Jules slapped Manfred on the back and the three

men walked ahead of the women back to the boarding house.

At the boarding house, Lottie Mae had trouble keeping her mind on her tasks and her eyes off Manfred. She'd never had this trouble before. It was frustrating.

Darie had refused to go to the church with them. She'd remained in the house, setting the table and finishing many of the chores that the other women usually did when they came home from church. With all the chores done, Lottie Mae found herself and Manfred along with everyone except Mrs. Dearling and Darie, sitting in the parlor waiting for dinner to be announced.

Lottie Mae hoped Manfred didn't realize how the other women, along with Beau and Jules, had managed to seat the two of them on the settee while everyone else sat in separate chairs. While she enjoyed being close to the man, she didn't want to think everyone was throwing him at her or her at him. Even though she knew his feelings and was beginning to realize hers.

The small talk in the parlor was hard to follow while she sat next to Manfred. She picked up pieces of what people were saying but didn't really hear anything as her shoulder rubbed his and his thigh touched her knee.

"Lottie Mae what do you think of the fact they are thinking about hiring another teacher at the school?" Beau asked.

Lottie Mae shook her head and looked at him. "What- what did you say?"

Beau and Jules both had grins on their faces. Beau said, "There are so many children living in Shady

Gulch now and with Miss Walker having left, they are looking for another teacher at the school. Have you thought about applying?"

Fear gripped Lottie Mae. Her hands shook as she stared at Beau. He knew why she couldn't apply for that job. Why was he bringing it up now, here, in front of Manfred? She shook her head and felt Manfred shifting closer to her.

"Ja, Miss Lottie, you should try for the teaching position," Manfred said.

Lottie Mae glared at Beau. Then she turned to Manfred, and said, "I'm not ready to teach at a school."

Manfred studied her with a frown on his face. "You are a good teacher. You are teaching me."

"It's different teaching one person. Teaching an adult. Someone who doesn't—" She stopped before she said something that she would regret. She stood. "I'm going to help in the kitchen." She left the room and hurried into the kitchen. She wasn't ready to tell Manfred why she couldn't teach at the school. She wasn't ready to tell Manfred why she wasn't worthy of him.

Manfred watched Lottie Mae walk out of the parlor in a hurry. He turned to Beau and asked, "What did I say wrong?"

Beau's reaction was one of sorrow. The owner of the saloon shook his head and said, "You didn't say anything wrong. Lottie Mae has some fears she needs to conquer. Her teaching you will help."

The other ladies in the room nodded their heads and murmured yes.

Manfred studied them all. They knew Lottie's past.

They knew what her fears were. He hoped that soon she would feel comfortable enough with him to tell him her fears and her past.

Mrs. Dearling came to the parlor door and announced dinner was ready. They all wandered into the kitchen where there was a long table with benches along the sides for everyone to sit.

This was the first time Manfred had been invited to have Sunday dinner with the people of the boarding house and the saloon. Even though he'd always thought saloon owners were on the shady side, he'd come to learn that Beau and Jules were men of integrity and treated the women that worked for them with respect.

Watching the group during the meal, he realized they were like a big family. The women looked up to Beau like a father or brother figure, Jules as a brother figure, and Mrs. Dearling as a mother figure. He liked the way they visited and bantered back and forth, and how they easily joked and teased. Having a meal with this group was showing him another side of Miss Lottie. A side he very much would like to see her show him.

The sad part of the meal was watching the new little woman, Darie. She didn't smile and didn't enter into any of the conversations or joking and teasing. She looked like a little wounded bird. Manfred wondered who the man was that had hurt her and hoped that when the man did show up, he would be able to show the coward what it was like to be on the other end of a beating.

When the meal ended, Lottie Mae asked him to wait for her in the parlor. When she returned, she had her books and slate. She tied a bonnet on her head. "I'm ready to go to the park."

They stepped out the door and he crooked his elbow, offering it to her. She slipped her hand through. He was the luckiest man on this earth to have such a pretty woman on his arm.

They took the long way to the park, walking slow and leisurely along the wood boardwalks as if they were man and wife or were courting. He felt like a king with this woman on his arm. Nothing would make him happier than to make her happy.

When they reached the park, he led her over to the bench where they had sat the other day. He brushed it off with his hands.

"Manfred, I have never been with a man who has treated me so nicely." Lottie Mae looked up at him with the brightest eyes he'd ever seen. His heart hammered in his chest and his hands shook as he raised one to push a strand of her loose hair behind her ear.

"Miss Lottie, all I want to do is make you happy."

They sat on the bench and started on his vocabulary. An hour into the lesson, Mr. Dentz arrived to pick up his plow.

"I need to go help Mr. Dentz load the plow. I will be right back." Manfred stood, setting the reader he'd been reading on the bench.

"Will this happen every Sunday or every time we sit down to work on lessons?" Lottie asked.

"No. I hope it does not. But I promised Mr. Dentz I would help him load his plow after church." While he didn't like to be the one to put the disappointment on Lottie's face, it made him happy that she was disappointed he had to leave so soon.

"If you would like to come watch, it would be fine." He offered his hand to her. She placed her hand in his, and he helped her stand. He released her hand as they walked over to his shop.

Mr. Dentz and his family all sat in the wagon waiting for him to arrive to help load the farm equipment.

Walking up to the wagon, Manfred said, "Mr. and Mrs. Dentz, this is my friend, Miss Lottie Mae."

"Miss Lottie." Mr. Dentz tipped his hat to her and Mrs. Dentz nodded her head. The children studied her.

"Ja, she is the woman who is helping you learn English," Mr. Dentz said.

"Yes," said Lottie. "I am helping Mr. Albrecht learn to speak English better and to read and write English."

Lottie Mae was happy to see that the Dentz family didn't treat her differently. She stood to the side with Mrs. Dentz as Manfred and her husband dragged the heavy farm implement out of the shop. Using a chain and a pulley, they lifted the implement. Mr. Dentz drove his wagon underneath the plow while Manfred held it. Hand over hand, he lowered the implement into the back of the wagon.

She'd never seen a man with such strength before. Her belly did crazy flips and fluttering, witnessing the bulging of Manfred's upper arms. She glanced over at the woman standing beside her and noticed she was also impressed by Manfred's muscles. Lottie Mae knew the woman loved her husband, however, that didn't snuff the jealousy that tweaked her good mood.

Once the plow was in the wagon and Mr. Dentz had paid Manfred, the family climbed back into the wagon. Mr. Dentz shook hands with Manfred and the two parted.

Manfred walked over to Lottie Mae, grinning.

"What are you grinning about?" she asked.

"Mr. Dentz said I am a very lucky man to have such a pretty school teacher." Manfred held out his dirty hands. "I will go wash my hands. Do you wish to wait here or walk back to the park?"

Lottie Mae was pleased that Mr. Dentz complementing her pleased Manfred. Being curious about where he lived she said, "If you don't mind I will wait here."

Manfred looked around, and then nodded his head towards the door of his shop. "Follow me. I do not think it will be improper for you to wait inside while I wash my hands." Manfred held the door, and she walked through it.

The first room they walked through housed tools and various sizes and shapes of iron. Some that had been forged into usable implements and others that were waiting to be manipulated. Manfred opened the door at the back of this room and motioned for her to go first.

She stepped into a small room with a potbelly stove, a chair and small table, and a much longer, wider cot than any she had ever seen. A trunk sat at the foot of the cot and some of Manfred's clothes hung from metal hooks on the wall. There was a small washstand and a mirror on the wall at the end of the bed.

Manfred walked over to the washstand and poured water into the basin. He washed his hands while Lottie Mae continued to study the room, taking in all she could about the man.

She felt sorry for Manfred living in one room such as this. But she also lived in one room, though she did have access to all of the boarding house. Even though they were so different, they were very much alike.

Manfred turned toward her, wiping his hands on a towel. He smiled and shrugged. "It is not much. But one day I hope to have a home."

"Where do you plan to build your new home?" Lottie Mae walked two steps closer to him.

Manfred hung up the towel and met her. "I would like a little place outside of town. One where I could keep a few animals, be able to tend to my work, and raise a family." He peered down into her face. "What do you wish for?"

"I would like to live outside of town, but close enough I can walk to the store or the school. I would like a small house. I would like children." Her heart squeezed as she gazed into his eyes and saw a twinkle in their depths. "And I would like a husband who treats me with respect."

He frowned. His hands came up to cup both sides of her face. His brown eyes gazed into hers. "Other than a man who will give you respect, which you should always have, what else must you have in a husband?"

Her heart banged around inside of her chest as her face warmed under his gentle palms. Her body moved closer to his. When she realized the inches separating them, she straightened her spine to stop the movement. Before her mind overrode her emotions, she spouted what her heart wanted. "I think I would like a man just like you."

Manfred's grin grew slowly. He lowered his head

and touched his lips to hers in a brief chaste kiss. He straightened, peering into her eyes and said, "You, Miss Lottie, would make me the happiest man if that comes true."

The jangling of harnesses and heavy thump of the wheels of a freight wagon rolling down the street jarred her from the thoughts that were going through her head. She stepped back, putting space between them.

"I think we need to get back to studying." She spun on her heel and walked to the door. Manfred's heavy footsteps followed behind her. She hurried through his blacksmith shop and out into the street. A glance over at the park revealed children running around the bench where they had left the slate and reader.

"Oh no! I left all the supplies sitting on the bench." She hurried across the street, her skirt flapping around her ankles, to retrieve the school supplies. Before she reached the bench, Manfred had passed her and was talking to the children. Lottie Mae knew Manfred would be good with children. How good she didn't know until she watched him cajole the slate away from a little girl and talk a little boy into handing him the reader.

"These are my school studies," he said to the children.

"You study?" The little girl asked Manfred.

"Ja, I do not speak good English. Miss Lottie is helping me speak better and to read and write English." Manfred glanced her direction and smiled.

Lottie Mae walked over to the bench and sat down. She held out her hand.

Manfred handed her the slate.

She glanced around and found the chalk laying on the ground by the bench. She retrieved the chalk and printed out the alphabet on the slate. "How many of you know what these are?" she asked.

"I do!" the little boy exclaimed. "I go to school. My little sister don't."

"Doesn't. My little sister doesn't," she corrected him. "That's because she's not old enough to go to school yet." She studied the pouting little girl. "But you look like a smart little girl to me. Would you like to sit here and learn the alphabet with Manfred?"

The little girl nodded her head and grinned.

Manfred sat down on the bench beside Lottie Mae and picked the little girl up, placing her on his lap. Together the two of them learned about the sounds the letters made, and soon they were both reading the first page in the reader. Lottie smiled at them. Manfred was a natural with children. He would be a very good father.

"Sarah! Sarah, what are you doing?" A woman marched down the street toward the park. "Timmy, why did you and Sarah run off?" The woman continued her forceful strides right up to the bench and thrust her hands on her hips. She glared at Lottie Mae. "What are you doing with this woman?"

Manfred placed the little girl on the ground. He looked down at the woman. "Miss Lottie is teaching Sarah and I the alphabet and how to read." He loomed over the woman.

She backed up a bit, but her expression remained hostile. "Come children! Come with me now." The woman gathered the boy and the girl to her and herded them down the street.

Just as Lottie Mae was thinking that life could be

different, she was shown how others would always see her. The other woman's scorn had shaken her confidence.

Manfred sat back down and put his hand over her hand on the reader. "Don't let that woman bother you. She knows nothing about you. She doesn't know your heart or how you can help people learn."

Lottie Mae peered into the man's face. If they did live outside town, she wouldn't have to come to town and be subjected to the criticism of the townsfolk.

Manfred removed his hand, settled back on the bench, and opened up the reader. He began reading, and she forgot all about the woman as she listened to his warm voice and helped him with the words.

Chapter Ten

Lottie Mae entered the saloon, glanced at the bar, and wasn't surprised Manfred stood at the end. He'd been in every evening after dinner and stood at the end of the bar, sipping on one beer and visiting with her when she had a chance. He'd asked her about Darie and if she was excited for the social coming up tomorrow night. Lottie Mae was happy to tell him that Darie's dreams were getting better.

However, she'd had two nightmares herself in the last week. Both woke her. She wasn't sure if it was because her feelings were growing for Manfred and she feared telling him her past or because she'd turned in a resume to the school and feared they would find out about her past. No matter the reason for her dreams, she wanted to keep it all from Manfred. She still wasn't sure how or when she'd be able to tell him about her past.

"You're going to be the prettiest woman at the dance tomorrow night," Manfred said.

Lottie Mae smiled at him but shook her head. "I don't know about that. But if you keep coming in here visiting with me, people are going to talk."

Manfred just grinned. "I don't care what others think. I know I want to spend time with you. This is where you work."

Lottie Mae smiled back at him. "I'm sorry that my work takes up so much of my time. We have the social tomorrow night to visit and Sunday afternoon to work on your schooling."

He nodded. "Ja, I can hardly wait until I dance with you."

Her cheeks warmed, and her heart rat-a-tatted in her chest like a woodpecker trying to get out. This week she'd dreamt about dancing in Manfred's arms as she went about her chores. That she was so excited was good, but that her nightmares had come back, bothered her.

"Why are you frowning?" Manfred started to reach towards her. She took a step back.

She didn't want to hurt Manfred's feelings, but she didn't want him to touch her. Not here. Not in the saloon. She only wanted him to touch her as they had on Sundays when they walked like a married couple to the park and sat in the park where everyone could see their respectable behavior as she taught him.

Manfred dropped his hand to the counter alongside his mug. His gaze studied her face and he said, "I'm sorry. I forget."

She shook her head. "I'm the one who's sorry. If things were different, we wouldn't have to pretend and not show our feelings."

Beau walked down to the end where they stood. "Savannah said she wanted you to come over to her house tomorrow morning."

Lottie Mae looked at her boss. "Why would she need me to come over there tomorrow morning?"

Beau shrugged. "I don't know. I'm passing along what I was told." He wandered back down to the other end of the bar.

Why would Savannah want her to come by the house tomorrow? Could it have something to do with Darie? Lottie Mae stared at the bar, scrubbing at a stain with a towel.

"It will be good to see Mrs. Webster, Ja?" said Manfred.

She glanced up at his grinning face, narrowed her eyes, and studied him. "Do you know something about this?"

He just grinned, finished off his beer, and walked out the door.

Lottie Mae stared at Manfred's shadow in the window until a customer hollered he needed more to drink. She picked up a bottle and walked over to where the man stood at the bar.

"You sure been spending a lot of time talking to that big blacksmith." The man held up his whiskey glass, nodded at her, and downed the whole thing.

"What I do and don't do is none of your business." She placed the bottle on the counter in front of him, scooped up the money, and dumped it in the till. She wandered past Beau and said, "I'm taking a break."

She walked right on out of the bar, through the back room, and over to the boarding house. It was rare that she left the bar any time after dinner unless Darie had a nightmare. Tonight, she felt restless. She didn't want to be around all the men. She didn't want to pretend about anything.

Lottie Mae entered the parlor. Mrs. Dearling glanced up from her handiwork. Darie sat on the settee working on a piece as well.

"Are you ill?" Mrs. Dearling asked, putting her needlework to the side and standing.

"No, I'm just tired. Tired of working at the saloon." She sat down on the settee next to Darie and let out a huge sigh. "I want to teach. I want to teach and not work at a saloon. I want men to look at me like they look at other women in town."

Her landlady's eyes twinkled. "You have caught the eye of an eligible man. Tomorrow night you can dance to your heart's content at the social. When everyone sees how Manfred treats you with respect, they will, too."

Lottie Mae peered at the older woman. "How can you say that? What do you know?"

The older woman shook her head. "I only know the way people think and how you will act. The townsfolk will see you in a new way."

Darie spoke up. "I think you two are good together."

Lottie Mae studied the younger woman. That she approved of Manfred was a good sign. She had noticed that Darie was becoming more comfortable around Beau and Jules when they came to meals. "Thank you.

Manfred is the only man who I can see myself having a happy life with." Her cheeks burned with embarrassment that she had spoken the words out loud.

Mrs. Dearling clapped her hands. "I knew you two were getting along well. I can't wait for you to dance together tomorrow."

Lottie Mae stood, fluffed out her skirt, and headed to the door. "I guess I should get back to work. But I am getting tired of working at the saloon." She wandered out the back door, across the alley, and returned to the Silver Dollar.

Entering the saloon, she heaved a sigh and took her place back behind the bar. Beau walked over to her, bumped her shoulder with his, and said, "That position is still open at the school."

Lottie Mae scanned the men crowded into the building watching Freedom sing and told herself she was going to go through with the interview when the superintendent came to town. Just marrying Manfred wasn't going to get her the respectability she'd once had.

Manfred towel dried his wet hair and peered at his reflection. He'd gone to the bathhouse to get cleaned up and then the barber to get a good shave and a haircut. Now he stood in front of the mirror combing his hair and straightening his tie. He wished the flock of frightened geese flapping around inside his belly would quiet. He'd never been so nervous or excited in his life.

Knowing he could hold Lottie in his arms tonight as they danced had him happier than he'd ever been. Even though he'd received friendly joking from some of the men who had showed up at his shop the last couple of weeks for repairs and forge work, he didn't care. He'd made up his mind that Lottie Mae was the woman for him.

He knew there was something in her past that had put her in the saloon. She was such a good teacher, he knew it wouldn't be long before she'd be teaching in the school. Even if she didn't get the job, he was still going to ask her to marry him after they'd had a respectable courtship.

Manfred stepped out of his shop to walk over to the boarding house and escort Lottie Mae to the social.

The whistle blew for the return trip of the train from Bismarck. Who came and went on the train didn't concern him.

Manfred had traveled to Shady Gulch from Chicago in the baggage car of a train with his crated-up tools. Why he decided to start a blacksmith shop here, he'd never know. After losing his wife and child, he'd wanted to find a new place to start over. In that way, he and Lottie were alike.

He strode down the street toward the boarding house.

The sun set low in the sky as he walked up the front porch steps of the boarding house and knocked. A patter of many feet could be heard before the door opened.

Miss Belle stood on the other side of the open door. "Welcome Mr. Albrecht," she said.

Manfred's shirt collar felt as if it had shrunk. The woman made him nervous the way she looked him up and down, not opening the screen door.

"I-I-I'm here to pick up Lottie for the dance." He

couldn't believe how hard it was to say the words with his mouth feeling as if it were full of dust.

Miss Belle nodded and opened the screen door. "Come in. She'll be ready in a minute."

Manfred entered the house. Belle grabbed his sleeve, leading him into the parlor. All the other women, except Freedom, sat in the parlor, wearing their best dresses. He felt out of place among all the ruffles and lace.

Footsteps pattered down the stairs and into the parlor. Miss Freedom stopped just inside the door with a big smile on her face.

"Lottie Mae is ready for the dance," she said, waving her hand toward the doorway.

Air whooshed out of Manfred as if someone had thrown an anvil at his chest when Lottie Mae walked through the door. She wore an emerald green dress that sucked in at her waist, puffed out around her hips and had a high modest collar. Every inch of her was covered except for her hands, creamy neck, and her lovely face. And he didn't think he'd ever seen a more beautiful sight.

He walked over to her and smiled. He couldn't stop gazing at her shining face and glittering eyes. They held welcome and a glimmer of the fun they were going to have together.

"Are you ready Miss Lottie?" he asked.

Lottie's cheeks deepened in color and she smiled. She nodded her head. "I'm ready if you are Mr. Albrecht."

Manfred offered his arm and she tucked her hand in the crook of his elbow. He led her out of the house, down the steps, and around the corner to walk to the church.

The evening light was slowly fading as they walked up to the area in between the church and the Webster house where the dance was to take place. Planks had been placed on the ground like a big wooden dance floor. A wagon stood at one end of the platform. The musicians sat in the wagon, tuning up their instruments. Saw horses and lumber had been set up on one side of the dance floor for the refreshments.

As they walked up to the area, Lottie Mae exclaimed, "I forgot to bring the pie I baked!"

"I'm sure the others will bring it for you," Manfred said. He didn't want anything to keep them from sharing the first and the last dance.

Mrs. Webster, the Reverend's wife, hurried over to them. "Lottie Mae, I told you that dress would look wonderful on you." The woman grabbed Lottie by the hand and gave her a good looking over.

"I don't know how to thank you for allowing me to wear this dress tonight." Lottie Mae's eyes glistened with unshed tears.

Manfred now understood why the dress looked so wonderful on Lottie. It was one of Mrs. Webster's dresses. The woman had arrived in Shady Gulch with only a few, having fled a money hungry man who wished to marry her. Beau and Reverend Webster had saved Savannah from the man and discovered he had been holding back her inheritance. She married the Reverend and used her money to help the church and town. Manfred never did hear the whole story behind Beau's sister. However, she fit into the town just fine and knew everything about the women of the boarding house. They all treated her like a sister.

"Well, I need to get back to the refreshment table," Mrs. Webster said. "Did you make anything?"

"I did. But when Manfred picked me up, I completely forgot about bringing my pie." Lottie's gaze on his face made him feel like the richest man in the world.

"I told her the others would bring it along."

Savannah patted Lottie's arm. "That's true. Mrs. Dearling wouldn't leave your pie sitting on the counter." The woman walked over to the refreshment table to help people placing their food among the others.

The musicians finished warming up and started the first song.

Lottie Mae's heart sped up at the notes of a waltz. Before she could even ask Manfred if he'd like to dance, he swung her into his arms and onto the dance floor. He kept her at a respectful distance. They gazed into one another's eyes as they moved about the wooden floor, dipping and swirling to the music. She'd never been as comfortable or as happy in a man's arms as she was floating across the boards in Manfred's.

When the song finished and the next song was a folk dance, Manfred led her by the elbow over to the end of the refreshment table. He captured two cups of punch, and they stood to the side, watching the other dancers stomp, twirl, and clap to the music.

Lottie Mae had never had such a wonderful time at a dance. All the other socials that had happened while she was in Shady Gulch, she'd always stood by Mrs. Dearling, hoping no one would ask her to dance. Every time a waltz started, Manfred grasped her hand and led her onto the dance floor. She loved the motion of the dance, the fluid way the big man moved about the crowded area, and how she felt like a princess in this dress and in his eyes.

During the third dance when they were standing to the side of the dance floor, she noticed a man walking toward them. Manfred inched a little closer and the man spun around, hurrying away. She glanced up at her escort and he smiled.

When another man walked her direction, Manfred started talking to her, and the gentleman turned and walked away. She started giggling.

"What is funny?" Manfred asked, his eyes twinkling.

"All you have to do is move closer to me or talk to me when another man approaches and he tucks tail."

"They know I have eyes for you. And they know I am stronger than all of them." He made an imperious expression, and she fell into a fit of giggles. She pressed the back of her hand to her mouth and stared at him. She had never had this much fun as an adult. And she owed it all to the big man staring down at her as if she were the most precious gift he'd ever been given.

Lottie Mae was surprised by how many people attended the social. Many of the faces were familiar, either from visiting the Silver Dollar or attending church, and some were just faces that she had come to know around town. Many people she didn't know. It appeared the whole town, and people from miles outside of town, were attending the social. There were many new people as well. She imagined they were travelers who had gotten off the train in Shady Gulch.

She spotted Freedom dancing with Belle on the corner of the dance floor. Belle didn't care whether or not she danced with a man or ever had another one in her life. Freedom had been looking for a husband ever since Lottie Mae came to live in the boarding house. While many people didn't care for Freedom and her kind, Lottie Mae thought it would be nice if Manfred danced with her friend.

"Manfred, why don't you ask Freedom to dance?" Lottie Mae peered up into his big face.

"I would, but I don't want to leave you alone." Manfred glanced over at Freedom and back at her. "I think my dancing with you caught other men's attention."

She had to admit that she liked the big man standing next to her and dancing with her and didn't want anyone to approach her to dance. "You're tall. Do you see anyone Freedom could dance with?"

Manfred twisted and turned, looking all through the crowd. A smile tugged at his lips when he looked toward the refreshment table. "I have found a man for Freedom." He grasped Lottie Mae's hand and led her around the edge of the dance floor, his gaze speared to a spot by the refreshment table.

As soon as they stood at the end of the table, Lottie Mae noticed the man in the fringed shirt and buckskins. He had a large piece of Freedom's special shoo-fly pie on a plate. She grasped Manfred and exclaimed, "That's the man that bought her pie at the pie social!"

Lottie Mae headed toward the man with Manfred on her heels. She stopped a foot away and smiled before saying, "Would you care to dance with the woman who made that pie?"

The man's head swiveled toward her. A smile tipped up the edges of his lips. "Is she here?"

Lottie Mae nodded her head and pointed toward the corner of the dance floor where Freedom and Belle still danced.

The man handed his plate of pie to Lottie Mae. "Could you hold on to this until I come back?"

Lottie Mae nodded, taking the pie. She glanced up at Manfred. He had a big smile on his face. They stood together, Lottie Mae holding the pie, Manfred at her side, watching the man make his way through the crowd to Freedom.

The man tapped Freedom on the shoulder. She spun around, and her face lit up. The last thing Lottie Mae saw of the two, they waltzed onto the crowded dance floor.

Once they disappeared into the dancers, Manfred walked her back over to the refreshment table. Lottie Mae was anxious to see how Freedom and the man got along. She and Manfred had another glass of the punch and watched the dancers.

Beau strode toward them with Mrs. Dearling on his arm. He stopped beside them, staring into the dancing couples. "Is Freedom dancing with that man who bought her pie at the pie social?"

Lottie Mae nodded. "We saw him getting a piece of her pie and told him where to find her."

Beau shook his head but had a slight smile. "Are you two having a good time?" he asked.

"I am." Manfred said.

"I am, too." Lottie Mae smiled up at Manfred, and he winked at her.

"I believe everyone is having a good time," Mrs. Dearling said. She removed her hand from Beau's arm. "It looks as if I could help with the refreshment table." She wandered over to Savannah.

"Looks like I lost my dance partner. Guess I'll dance with my sister since Mrs. Dearling relieved her." He strode toward Savannah and the two were soon waltzing among the other dancers.

"You know he only wanted to dance to keep an eye on Freedom," Lottie Mae said.

"Why would he need to keep an eye on Freedom?" Manfred asked.

"I don't know if you've noticed, but some people don't take kindly to Freedom's kind." Lottie Mae had always had a hard time figuring out why some people were judged by their skin color, others by the way they talked, and others by the job they had.

"It's what's inside a person, not what you see on the outside," Manfred said.

His comment was one more reason she grew fonder and fonder of the man.

The musicians took a break. Manfred drew her a few feet away from the refreshment table as the thirsty dancers headed that direction.

"Keep an eye out for the man with Freedom. I'd like to hand him his pie."

Manfred nodded, and stared into the crowd.

Freedom and her dance partner emerged from the crowd, both had smiles on their faces and their steps were light.

"There they are! There they are!" Freedom pointed towards them.

Freedom hurried over with the man following.

They stopped in front of Manfred and Lottie Mae. The man held out a hand and Lottie Mae placed his pie in it.

"Thank you for saving this for me. I darn sure didn't want to lose this piece. It's the best shoo-fly pie I ever had." He smiled down at Freedom and took a bite of the pie.

Even though Freedom's skin was a dark brown, her cheeks became even darker as she blushed. "Ben said he's going to be coming through this way more often." The excitement in her friend's voice made Lottie Mae happy. She wanted Freedom to find happiness with a husband and children. She knew her friend didn't have the fear of men like everyone else in the boardinghouse. Her problem and how she'd come to have Beau as her benefactor had to do with her coloring.

"When the musicians start playing again, we need to dance," Manfred said.

Lottie Mae agreed. They hadn't spent enough time dancing.

When the music filled the air once more, they started with a waltz. Manfred led her out onto the dance floor. They were soon both lost in the pleasure of being so close and moving as one. Lottie Mae's eyes were closed as she moved to the sounds of the music and Manfred's gentle grip on her hand and her waist.

Manfred stopped, but the music still played. She opened her eyes.

A man stepped from behind Manfred and her heart lodged in her throat. He was five years older, but there was no mistaking the curly blonde hair, crooked nose, and the coldness in his eyes.

Manfred must have witnessed fear in her eyes. He

spun around, placing his body between her and the man. "What do you want?" Manfred asked in a hard tone she'd not heard from him before.

She couldn't see Thomas, but just the sound of Manfred's voice turned her blood cold.

"I wanted to dance with the lady."

"No one dances with her but me." Manfred pulled her under his arm, and they walked off the dance floor.

Her heart thumped in her chest. Darie! Did the man know that she was here? Lottie Mae didn't know whether to run to the house, find Beau, or just leave. Manfred's strong arm around her shoulders held her next to him. His strength and warmth kept her from bolting. He led her over to Beau. When they stopped, she glanced at Beau and knew the shock and fear of seeing Thomas still lingered on her face.

"What happened?" Beau closed the distance between her and Manfred in two strides.

"A man asked to dance with her." Manfred glanced down at her. "As soon as she saw him her face turned white."

Beau moved closer, peering into her eyes. "What man?"

She shook her head. She didn't want to talk about it here. Not in front of Manfred. "The house. We need to get to the house." She glanced up at Manfred. "I had a wonderful time. But I must go now."

Manfred shook his head. "I will walk you to the boarding house."

"As will I." Beau stepped to the other side of her.

The two tall, broad-shouldered men escorting her away from the churchyard made her feel safe. However, knowing the depth of Thomas's mean streak, she peered back over her shoulder several times hoping she didn't catch a glimpse of him. When they reached the boarding house, Beau stepped inside giving her and Manfred a minute alone.

Manfred put a hand on her cheek, "I don't know who that man is, but I know he has hurt you. I will not let him or anyone else hurt you again."

She turned her head and kissed his warm, wide palm before stepping away "Thank you, Manfred. I know you would never hurt me. But I have a past I need to tell you about but not now. Not tonight. I must go to Darie."

As she put her hand on the door latch, Manfred touched her shoulder, stopping her.

"I will be ready to hear whenever you are ready to tell me. Nothing you say will change how I feel about you."

Lottie Mae opened the door and whispered, "I hope that is true."

Chapter Eleven

Lottie Mae walked into the house and found Beau and Darie sitting at the kitchen table waiting for her. She paced from the kitchen door to the back door, spun and paced back again. She didn't know how to tell Darie that her worst fear had arrived in Shady Gulch. Knowing Beau, once he found out about the man, it would be hard to keep him out of jail. Not only had Thomas violated Darie, he'd violated her as well.

"Lottie Mae, sit down." Beau motioned to the bench next to Darie.

Lottie Mae shook her head. She didn't know what to say. She didn't know what to do. Another thought struck her. "Just when I wanted to go back to teaching, he shows up."

"You can still go back to teaching. What are you talking about?" Beau asked, again, motioning to the bench.

Lottie Mae continued pacing.

"What is wrong, Lottie Mae?" Darie asked in a soft voice.

Lottie Mae glanced down at the young woman. Her bruises were nearly gone, the scratches had healed, and she had smiled a couple times today as everyone was bustling around getting ready for the social. Why now? Why did he have to show up now?

She sat down on the bench next to Darie. Lottie Mae couldn't look at the young woman.

"He's here," she said to Beau. "The man who attacked Darie." She drew in a full breath and let it out on a huge sigh. "He is also the same man who attacked me five years ago." Once the words came out, she stared at the table.

Darie rose and cried, "He'll kill me!"

Beau put a hand on the young woman's shoulder, easing her back down on the bench. "No one will hurt you." He tapped Lottie Mae's hand, getting her to look at him. "How do you know the same man hurt both you and Darie?"

She repeated what Darie had told her and how she'd hoped it wasn't the same person, but after seeing him tonight, she knew he was one and the same. A thought froze her heart. "He's still out there!"

Beau narrowed his eyes. "What do you mean?"

"He will hurt another woman if he stays here. He could also discover Darie is here." The fear she felt for Darie and other women overrode her fear for herself. "You have to get him out of town." She shot to her feet.

"Stay. You and Darie stay here. Manfred knows

what he looks like. We'll escort this man…"

"Thomas, Thomas Decker."

"This Decker to the jail and make sure he's on the next train out of Shady Gulch." Beau stood and peered down at them. "Stay in this house. I'll send Mrs. Dearling to be with you."

"No. Don't ruin her night. We'll be fine until everyone comes home." Lottie Mae put a hand on Darie's.

He nodded and headed out the back door.

Manfred had gone to his home after leaving Lottie. But it didn't feel right that she was cooped up in the boarding house while the man who had scared her walked free. He peeled off his good coat and necktie and plopped his work hat onto his head to go back to the dance and keep an eye on the man.

Out in the street, he spotted a familiar form striding toward him.

"Manfred. Come with me to find the man who scared Lottie Mae. I want to put him in jail until the train comes through tomorrow." Beau pivoted and headed back the way he'd come.

Manfred fell into step beside him. "Why does this man scare Lottie?"

Beau shook his head. "It's not my story to tell. She'll tell you when she's ready. All I can say…he is the man who hurt Darie and threw her off the train."

Anger sizzled up Manfred's spine and fisted his hands. Remembering the bruises, scratches, and fear on Darie when he first met her, he could only imagine what the stranger must have done to Lottie Mae to have her fearful of the man.

"I would help you if you wanted to castrate him."

Beau chuckled. "We might do that if he doesn't stay out of our town and away from our women."

At the dance, Manfred was glad he was so tall. He scanned the crowd and found the man dancing with the oldest daughter of the café owner. "There he is, dancing with Sigrid Pedersen."

Beau shouldered his way through the dancers with Manfred following in his wake. The saloon owner grabbed the man by his arm, jerking him away from the young woman.

"What are you doing?" the man snarled and swung a fist toward Beau.

Manfred grabbed the arm and between the two of them, they carried him with his feet several inches from the ground, off the dance floor.

"Where are you taking me?" the man hollered.

The people attending the dance stopped, as did the music. Manfred continued when Beau showed no sign of letting the man go.

They marched him down the street and into the Sheriff's Office. Manfred was surprised to find Sheriff Blake in the office and not attending the social.

"What are you doing carrying that man around?" Sheriff Blake asked, standing and placing a hand on the gun in his holster.

"I have two reliable people who say the women of this town aren't safe with this man here." Beau shoved the stranger toward Sheriff Blake. "I would like you to keep him in the jail until the train comes through tomorrow on its way to Fargo."

Sheriff Blake shook his head and grasped the

stranger by the arm. "Are you sure about this, Beau?"

Manfred couldn't keep quiet any longer. He stepped forward. "I also know the person who is fearful of this man. I agree with Beau. Put him on the train and get him out of our town." The fear he'd witnessed in Lottie's eyes was all he needed to know the man was no good.

He took a step toward the Sheriff and the stranger. "If you don't put him in jail, I will." Manfred stuck his hand out to grab the man by the collar.

Sheriff Blake jerked the man away from Manfred and toward the jail cell.

"Don't I have a say before I get thrown in jail?" the stranger asked.

"Not in this town." Beau took a step toward the man.

"I think you'd be a lot safer in jail, mister, with the anger blazin' in those two's eyes. And head out of town tomorrow on the train." Sheriff Blake led the stranger to the back cage of iron bars. He opened the door, shoved the man in, then closed and locked the door.

"You can't do this! You can't throw an innocent man in jail." The stranger banged on the iron and hollered.

Sheriff Blake followed Manfred and Beau outside. Once they were all standing out on the boardwalk, he said, "I sure hope you two know what you're doing."

"If you saw the fear in Lottie Mae's eyes when she looked at that man..." Manfred's hands fisted. If he could get his hands on the stranger in the jail cell, he would not be able to let go.

"Lottie Mae said this is the man who caused her to lose her job five years ago, and she believes he is the same man who attacked Darie on the train a month ago. The description and the first name fit him." Beau crossed his arms. He glared at the sheriff.

Sheriff Blake ran a hand over his face. "I know better than to go against you when it comes to protecting the women in your boarding house. It's like banging my head against the wall. But if he comes back here with an attorney and wants to cause trouble, I'm not going to stand in his way." Sheriff Blake spun on his heel and marched back into the jail.

Manfred stared at the closed door. How could the sheriff, a man who had sworn to protect the townsfolk, allow such a creature as the one in his cell to have privileges?

"Come on, I'll buy you a drink." Beau slapped Manfred on the back and headed across the street to the Silver Dollar.

Manfred fell into step alongside the saloon owner. The saloon had been closed so everyone, including the women, Beau, and Jules could attend the social. He knew the other saloons in town were still open tonight. The Silver Dollar was run more like a family owned business than the other disreputable saloons.

Not much of a drinker, Manfred realized he needed a drink to calm the anger. They entered through the front door and Beau lit a lantern before he walked behind the bar and poured a jigger of whiskey and a mug of beer. He nodded to a table, and they both sat down.

"I know Lottie Mae hasn't told you what brought her here. But I can tell you this much, that man over in the jail was one of the reasons." Beau threw back the jigger of whiskey and returned to the bar, grabbing the bottle.

On second thought, Manfred wasn't sure drinking the beer would help douse the anger boiling in his chest. He didn't like to think about anyone hurting Lottie Mae. "I know something terrible happened to her. Something that makes her fearful of men." The beer loosened his lips. "She likes you and Jules." He grinned, "I think she's beginning to like me, too."

"Yes, she is beginning to like you very much," Beau agreed.

"That makes me a happy man." Manfred took another sip of the beer and pictured Lottie humming and busying herself around a small house on the outskirts of town.

Beau studied him. "We'll need to keep an eye out for that weasel over in the jail. Even if he's put on the train tomorrow headed east, there's no guarantee he won't come back."

"Ja, I feel the same. If he is a mean man who attacks women, he will want to hurt those who know it." Repulsion for the man and fear for Lottie Mae sent tremors through his body.

"I'll have Jules go over and take a look at the man in the morning, before he's put on the train. That way the three of us and Ty will know to keep an eye out for him." Beau took a sip of whiskey. "I think I'll have one of the Flanagan boys also get a look at him. I'll pay him to meet the train every day and watch to see if the man gets off."

Manfred nodded. "That is a good idea. We need to know if that skunk is around."

Beau stood and held out his hand. "Then we're in

agreement. Keep an eye out for this man and keep Lottie Mae and Darie safe."

Manfred shook hands. "Ja, we will keep the women safe."

Chapter Twelve

Lottie Mae and Darie sat at the table in the kitchen, waiting for the other women to come home from the social. Lottie Mae wished she could have spent more time in Manfred's arms dancing, but she was safer here than out in the open where Thomas could find her. While she worried about Darie's safety, she also was angry that he had shown up now, when she was feeling better about herself and her life and getting ready to attempt teaching again.

"I say he's come here looking for me," Darie whispered.

"Beau and Manfred won't let him hurt you," Lottie Mae said, placing a hand on the young woman's shoulder.

The door opened. Voices and footsteps heralded the arrival of the other women who lived in the house.

Their voices carried down the hall and into the kitchen.

Mrs. Dearling stopped inside the room and studied the two. "Oh my, why such long faces after such a fun evening?"

Belle stepped forward. "I bet this has something to do with that stranger Beau and Manfred escorted away from the dance floor."

Lottie Mae studied her friend. "Was it a man with curly blonde hair and a crooked nose?"

Belle nodded. "Yes, and he didn't seem very happy with them."

Lottie Mae was happy to know the two men had taken her word about Thomas being dangerous to others. "Did you all see the man?"

Freedom stepped forward. "I didn't see him, I was dancing with Ben." Her eyes were all starry and a smile brighter than usual lit up her face.

"I'm glad you had a good time, Freedom. The man that Manfred and Beau escorted away from the dance is someone to stay away from. He is one of the young men who attacked me five years ago." She glanced at Darie to see if she would allow her to tell them the truth about the man. "May I tell them?"

Darie's eyes widened. Her gaze traveled from woman to woman before settling on Lottie Mae. She nodded.

"He is the same man who attacked Darie and threw her off the train."

All the women exclaimed and rushed forward, surrounding the two with comfort and security. The back door opened.

Beau and Manfred walked in. Beau nodded to

Manfred. He walked through the kitchen and down the hallway. "Lottie Mae, Manfred would like to talk to you in the parlor." Beau walked over and helped her to her feet. He peered into her eyes. "And I think it's time you told him everything."

Lottie Mae started to shake her head.

"He needs to know and not make up things in his head. He already knows the man has hurt you. You need to tell him what happened." He knelt next to Darie. "The man is in jail right now. Sheriff Blake will put him on a train tomorrow. After the man has left, I would like to take you to Sheriff Blake and have you tell him what happened."

Darie's head started shaking. Her face turned white. "I can't. I can't."

Lottie Mae put a hand on the young woman's shoulder. "Darie, if we can get Sheriff Blake to keep Thomas out of town, he isn't going to hurt someone we know and possibly us again."

Darie stared into her eyes for a long time and finally gave one short, slow nod.

Lottie Mae let out a relieved sigh and left the kitchen, heading to the parlor. She entered the room and found Manfred staring out the front window with his back to the door. She walked softly across the room.

He turned just as she came abreast of him. "It is time you told me everything." He placed a palm against her cheek, and she leaned into it.

"It's going to be hard to tell you. But I know you have a generous heart." She grasped his hand, leading him over to the settee. She sat, drawing him down beside her. Their arms and legs touched as he continued to hold onto her hand.

Lottie Mae swallowed the lump in her throat. Although she had told the story many times over the years, first to Beau, then Mrs. Dearling, and each woman as they had arrived at the house, telling the man staring at her with concern and caring in his eyes, her stomach clenched, and her throat tightened. The others were a man who had compassion for downtrodden women and women who had gone through similar situations. Telling Manfred, someone she had come to admire and care for, could mean losing his trust and faith in her. And losing him would feel as if she'd lost her family all over again.

Manfred leaned back, staring at the bookcase on the opposite wall. "Is it better if I do not look at you?"

"Honestly, I don't know." Lottie Mae stared at the man's profile. He would never judge her for something that wasn't her fault. Getting up the courage, she slowly and softly told her story.

Manfred listened to Lottie. His heart ached for what she had gone through. Fear, anger, and humiliation flashed across her face as she spoke. The man sitting in a jail cell had caused this beautiful woman with a generous and kind soul to feel as if she was worthless. Even more frustrating, he had not done the deed alone. It took all of his control to keep his anger at the man from scaring Lottie.

At the same time, he wondered that no one, not even her family had stuck up for her. Why? Had she been a young woman who rendezvoused with men? Or had acted flirtatious or a woman of loose morals?

These questions bombarded his mind, confusing his anger.

She finished, tears trickled down her cheeks as she peered up at him. "If you don't want to have anything to do with me because I am a ruined woman, I will understand."

Manfred stared into her tear puddled eyes and saw a scared woman. While he still wasn't sure about his feelings over her past, he could never ignore a crying woman.

He wrapped his arms around her and held her tight. He breathed in and out calmly, tamping the rage he wanted to unleash on the man who'd caused Lottie to think no man would want her and to think of words to say that would soothe. "You are not a ruined woman. You are a strong woman with a caring heart." He thought a moment. "If you have taught yourself this well to overcome your troubles, you will make a good teacher."

They sat in an embrace, her head against his chest, as footsteps tapped on the stairs, doors opened and closed, and the night grew quiet around them. This was a moment that had Lottie not told him of her past, he would have cherished. While he admired her strength to tell him what would make most men run from her or treat her differently, he had questions. He did believe there were bad men. Men who took advantage of women and treated them poorly. And having witnessed Lottie at the saloon, he wondered if her coldness to men was because her promiscuousness had somehow lured the young men to think she would accept their advances. He shook his head. It didn't make sense.

He thought perhaps if he showed Lottie how his actions of selfishness had lost him everything, she might reveal if she had felt she provoked the attack. He drew out of the embrace and held her by the shoulders, staring into her eyes.

"You are not the only one who has sorrow from a past. I had a wife. Her name was Nina. She was a fragile little bird. I loved her deeply. I wished to have children with her. But my selfishness made me lose everything." He swallowed hard, trying to tell the story without bringing back the sadness and horrific memories.

Lottie Mae put a hand over his and stared into his eyes. "You are too gentle of a man to have caused your wife's death."

"No, it is true. I said too much of wanting children. If I had kept my thoughts to myself, she would still be alive. The doctor said the baby was too big and she was too small. They both died that night as I sat out in the barn thanking God for giving me my Nina and a boy."

This time Lottie Mae wrapped her arms around Manfred. Her soft body and sweet-smelling hair reminded him of all the nights he slept alone. All the intimate touches and embraces he'd yearned for since burying Nina.

"You would never intentionally hurt anyone. There was no way you could know that she was unable to have your children." She leaned back, her gaze on him. "I would be honored to have your children. No matter the pain."

Manfred studied the woman in front of him. He saw the truth in her eyes. She was not fragile. She had lived through her attack and had become stronger. And she would make a fine mother.

Loneliness almost had him asking her to marry

him. Even as his body enjoyed the contact, his head told him to wait. Wait to see what else he could learn about the woman. His heart couldn't take another heartache.

"I'll keep that in mind when I am ready to take a wife to my bed again."

Lottie's eyes softened, and a smile graced her lips. "Manfred, you are the only one I would ever want to lay down beside. You are the only man I could ever trust with my body."

Mrs. Dearling stepped into the parlor. "I believe it is time for you to leave Manfred," the older woman said, motioning to the door.

Manfred knew Mrs. Dearling's rules. He was lucky the woman had allowed him this much time alone with Lottie. He stood, drawing Lottie Mae to her feet. "I will see you tomorrow at church, ja?"

"Yes, you will. And I would like you to sit with me." Lottie Mae led him out of the parlor to the front door.

"I would be honored to sit with you." He grasped his hat on the rack by the door, put it on his head, and walked outside. Tonight, he'd witnessed the real Lottie Mae. While he'd known her past wasn't pleasant because she worked in a saloon, he still had to think about the reason behind her downfall.

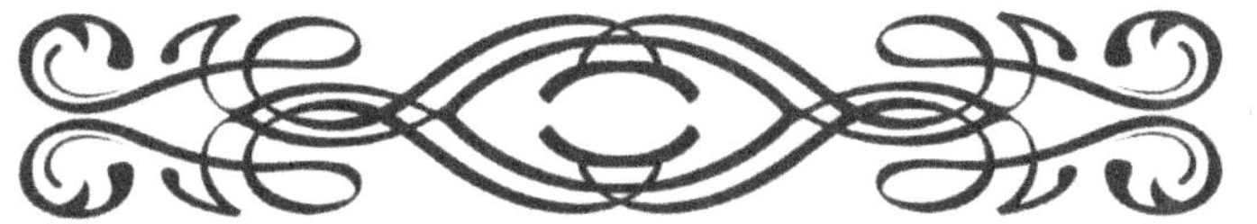

Chapter Thirteen

Lottie Mae was nervous Sunday morning. She knew that Thomas would be put on the train, however, she also knew he could get off at any stop and return by horseback to Shady Gulch. He knew she lived in this town. She hoped he didn't know Darie was here as well. While he hadn't threatened her, he had threatened the young woman. He had to know that someone told Manfred and Beau about how he treated women and that was why he was put in jail the night before. He would realize she had been the one, and to do that, she would have told what he and his friends did to her. She remembered him as a student and knew he held grudges and thrived on hurting others.

She was happy that Manfred didn't find her tainted by what had happened to her years ago. That he had confided in her his sorrow, had only made them grow closer.

Lottie Mae and Mrs. Dearling were finishing the last of the breakfast dishes when someone knocked on the front door.

"I'll see who it is," Freedom said, rushing out of the kitchen.

"It's too early for Beau, and he doesn't knock," Mrs. Dearling commented.

Freedom returned. Her usual smile and temperament had been even more joyful this morning. "You have someone waiting for you in the parlor," she said to Lottie Mae.

Lottie Mae wiped her hands on her apron, untied the garment, and draped it over a chair. There was only one person who would come visit her. She smoothed her hair and walked down the hallway to the parlor.

Just as he had the night before, Manfred stood looking out the front parlor window, his back to the room. She walked up behind him and put a hand between his broad shoulders, enjoying the hard muscle under the palm of her hand.

Manfred turned and smiled. "I thought I would escort you to church."

His dark eyes studying her, made her feel like a young girl. Her belly fluttered. "That would be nice. Would you like a cup of coffee? It's a bit early to walk to church."

"I thought, if you're ready, we could take a walk through the park before services." His eyes held a twinkle of mischief.

She smiled. "That would be wonderful. I'll get my bonnet."

He continued to peer into her eyes. The warmth

and desire in their brown depths had her stomach doing flipflops.

Her cheeks heated, and she ducked away from his gaze. "I'll be right back."

Climbing the stairs to her room, she fanned her face with one hand and settled the other over the sensations in her lower belly.

At the top of the stairs, she stopped short of running into Liesa.

"Are you rushing to be with Manfred?" Liesa asked.

She knew Liesa and Manfred had talked in their native German a few times. She wondered why Manfred preferred her over Liesa who was as pretty as a porcelain doll. Then she remembered how he'd spoken of his wife having been small and fragile. He would have seen her in Liesa.

"We are going for a walk in the park before church." Lottie Mae didn't continue to her room. She studied her friend. "You have talked with Manfred, is he as honorable as he seems?"

Liesa nodded her head. "He likes you very much. He would never do anything wrong. This I know from speaking to him." She smiled. "When two people are in love, everyone around them can tell." Liesa stepped around her. Before she headed down the stairs, she said, "Have a nice walk."

Lottie Mae twirled in the hallway and headed to her room for her bonnet and reticule. A walk under the trees and listening to the birds with Manfred, would be a wonderful way to start the day.

In the park, Lottie Mae was surprised to see so

many people out for an early morning stroll. She'd hoped they would have the area to themselves.

As if sensing her unease, Manfred led her away from the park and toward the livery. "Shall we take a buggy ride instead?"

"Yes, that would be wonderful." She clung to his arm as he escorted her down the street.

At the stable, she didn't care for the way Mr. Montgomery leered at her and told Manfred to take as long as he wanted with the buggy.

The buggy bumped across the railroad tracks as Manfred headed north.

"Where are we going?" she asked.

"There is a spring surrounded by trees not far from here." He pressed the horse into a trot.

"Will we be back in time for church?" she asked, unsure if she wanted rumors to spread that she'd missed church because she'd gone on a buggy ride with Manfred.

He glanced at her. "If you wish, we can turn around now, to make sure."

Her head said to tell him to turn around, but she enjoyed his company more than anyone back at town. "No, I'd like to see this place."

He smiled, and they continued.

She spotted trees in the distance. "Is that the place?" Anxious to see what kind of a spring would be out in the middle of this desolate country, she leaned forward on the seat.

"This place is special to me," Manfred said.

Lottie Mae glanced at him. His face appeared serene. "Why?"

He maneuvered the horse and buggy through the

copse of trees and stopped in a grassy spot alongside the spring. After setting the brake, he hopped down and held his arms up to her.

She dropped into his arms and within seconds her feet touched the ground and he had her arm wrapped around his.

"I purchased this land a week after I arrived here. It reminds me of my homeland. It is an oasis in the middle of harsh land."

Her heart thrummed in her chest. Was he showing her this because he was going to ask her to marry him? "It's beautiful. Will you build a home here?"

His gaze left the landscape and settled on her. "When I decide to marry again, I would like to build a house here, but I will keep my blacksmith shop in town."

Her heart picked up speed as his gaze roamed over her face. "Have you settled on the woman you wish to marry?"

He shook his head. "I am still thinking on this."

His answer stopped her pattering heart and had her belly aching as if she'd eaten a dozen green apples. Had her telling him about her past given him second thoughts about her as a wife? They'd been getting along well, and she'd seen interest in his eyes on more than one occasion.

She spun away from him before he saw sorrow on her face. Trying to not appear as if she were in a hurry, yet feeling the need to put space between them, she walked awkwardly toward the buggy. "We should get back before services begin."

Manfred didn't say anything, but she heard the

swishing of grass behind her, revealing he followed.

At the buggy, she grasped her skirt in one hand and the side of the buggy with her other to climb into the conveyance. Before she could hoist her body up, large hands grasped her waist, lifting her into the buggy.

"Thank you." She settled her skirt around her legs and waited for him to climb up.

When he was settled next to her, she scooted slightly away, so as not to touch him in any way. Now that she realized he was no different than other men, thinking the worst of her, she didn't want to touch him. Just the thought of not having him to talk with or—

"Do you still want me to teach you?" She wasn't sure if she wanted him to say yes. Could she endure spending time alone with him once a week and not have her heart yearning for him to think of her as a respectable woman and not a soiled one?

He'd set the buggy in motion, but pulled it to a stop at her question. "Why would I no longer want you to teach me?"

She felt foolish having to voice the thoughts in her head. Clearing her throat, forcing the lump of shame down, she said, "Knowing my past, I don't blame you for not wanting me to teach you."

Manfred grasped her chin, making her look at him. "The only thing I feel about what happened to you is anger at the young men."

Her heart skipped, fluttered, and pattered in her chest. "Really? You don't pity me or feel I'd not make a good wife?"

Manfred stared into her eyes. Hope lit the green orbs. What he wouldn't give to see those eyes full of happiness every day. But he had to know why the boys chose to attack her. He had to know, without a doubt, that she wasn't a woman of loose morals.

"I believe you are the only woman who would make me a happy man." He leaned down, closing the distance between their lips and felt her body shift toward his. Was this a reaction only to him?

He brushed his lips across hers.

Her soft mew of contentment heated his loins and nearly had him forgetting he needed to find out more before he let his mind, body, and heart allow this woman in.

She protested when he leaned back.

"Lottie, there's something I need to know."

Her heated gaze rose from his lips to his eyes. "What?"

He released her chin. Now that he'd started the conversation, he wasn't sure how to proceed. Just asking was going to make her mad. But he had to know the truth.

"There's something I can't figure out."

The heat turned to ice in her eyes. "What?"

"Don't take this wrong. I just don't understand three young men, students of yours, forcing themselves…" He couldn't say any more.

Her gaze became blank, her lips trembled. "You're just like my family. It had to be my fault. I had to have said or done something to make them think I wanted their advances." She reached for the side of the buggy as if to climb down.

"Don't." He grasped her arm.

She glared at him. "I don't want to be around you. I thought you were different. That you saw me as I am, not as others see me." She yanked her arm from his grasp and flung herself off the buggy.

"Get back in here!" he shouted as she ran toward the spring.

Chapter Fourteen

Lottie Mae held her skirt up and ran, looking for a place to hide and cry. She'd thought the big man with the soft heart was different. But he wasn't. He was like all the people back home who only believed she had to have provoked the three. She ducked behind a tree, sat on the ground, dropped her face into her hands, and sobbed. Her heart had never ached as it did at this moment.

She didn't want to work at the saloon forever. Her best chance at starting over was moving to a new place that was looking for a teacher. Some place that would be happy to have someone who had a certificate and not ask about references. But how did she go about finding such a place? Darie had been going somewhere to teach. She could show up in her place. The idea of leaving her friends at the boarding house saddened her, but she couldn't stay here knowing the one man she'd thought understood and believed her, didn't.

"Lottie? I'm sorry. I didn't mean…"

She stiffened hearing Manfred's voice. "I don't want to talk to you." Wiping at the tears on her cheeks, she turned her head away from his voice.

The sound of rustling grass and a soft thump told her he sat on the ground as well.

"I didn't mean to hurt you. I just can't imagine why?"

"You have mentioned that enough. Those three boys had been trouble from the moment I stepped into the school house. They were only a few years younger than me and acted as if I shouldn't be teaching them. I was forever having to reprimand them for disrupting the class." She wiped at her tears. "I did nothing to encourage them. They were my students, and I didn't really like them very much."

"Did they bother the girls in the class?"

"They tormented little Sally into tears nearly every day and her older sister acted afraid of the three. She wouldn't stand up for Sally. Just sat meekly in her seat and allowed the older boys to be mean." Lottie Mae turned to Manfred. She knew why the boys had attacked her. She'd been threatened that day and hadn't heeded it. That threat changed her life for the worse. "I'd told Thomas that day, that if he didn't leave Sally alone I was going to telegraph the superintendent and ask that he be removed from the school."

"Why the superintendent? Why not his father?" Manfred asked.

"Because his father refused to listen to me when I complained about the three boys." The events of the day, before she was attacked, were coming back in startling detail. "When I told Thomas about the telegraph, he threatened me. He said if I had him thrown out of school, he'd make sure I never taught again." She stared into Manfred's eyes. "They attacked me when I was walking home from sending the telegraph to the superintendent."

Manfred scooted toward her, closing the space between them. "My strong Lottie. You were hurt for doing what was right." He reached out to pull her into his arms.

She shoved against his chest. "When I gathered myself together and staggered home, my parents wouldn't listen to what I said. They pointed fingers at me and said I'd brought it on myself." Anger bubbled from within, hot and unpredictable as a boiling pot. "The superintendent never came. No one believed me that I'd been ruined because I wanted the three who'd attacked me out of my school. They, the boys, told everyone I'd lured them. I'd seduced them." Tears flowed down her cheeks. "I'd never been so humiliated. Felt so alone."

Manfred pulled her against his chest. "You'll never be alone again, *Schatzi*."

She didn't know what the word *schatzi* meant, but the way he said it, made her heart melt.

Lottie Mae snuggled into his embrace, believing him.

Now that Manfred knew the young men had attacked Lottie out of vengeance, he would put all his efforts into keeping her safe and making her his wife. He kissed her head and held her tight. She was a wonderful armful of soft woman. He inhaled her floral scent. His body stirred in a way it hadn't since Nina was alive. The sooner they became man and wife, the better. Or he would be the one to ruin her reputation.

Reluctantly, he released her. "We should return to town. As it is, we'll slip into the church late."

Lottie peered up at him from where her head rested on his chest. "Do we have to go? I would prefer sitting here with you to listening to Lark's sermon."

He would like nothing better than to remain with her. But being alone with Lottie and keeping his hands, and other body parts, away from her would be a test on his strength of character.

"I would like nothing more, *mien schatzi*. But being alone with you," he peered into her eyes as his hand rubbed up and down her arm, "could compromise you."

"What does that mean?" she said in a soft breathy voice.

The sound reminded him of making love to Nina. Her voice had sounded that way. The memory brought pain but also heightened his awareness of how Lottie leaned toward him.

"Compromise means—"

"No. I know what compromise means. What does *mien schatzi* mean? It sounds beautiful and fills my heart when you say it."

He chuckled. Had he known speaking to her in German filled her with joy, he would have used more words. "It means, my treasure."

Her eyes widened. "You think of me as a treasure?"

"Ja. You are a sparkling diamond that I have uncovered."

She leaned closer and pressed a chaste kiss to his lips. "Thank you. No one has ever said anything so wonderful to me."

"You, *mien schatzi*, are a gem of a teacher and a woman." He put a hand behind her head, shoving aside his reasons to keep his hands to himself, and drew her lips to his. He kissed her as he'd been dreaming of since the first night he'd worked as a bouncer in the Silver Dollar.

Lottie sighed when he drew out of the kiss. Her hands played with the hair at the back of his neck. "That was nice."

He grinned and stared into her eyes. "I'm glad you like my kiss."

"I have a feeling I'd like anything you did." Her cheeks darkened in a cute blush.

"I have the same feeling." He leaned in, kissing her again and restraining his hand from roaming where it shouldn't go. Not yet.

When he drew out of the kiss, she sighed again and leaned her head on his chest, pressing her upper body against his.

He enjoyed her trust in him, but having her soft breasts pressed against his chest and the sweet scent of her hair igniting his senses, he didn't know how long he could keep his hands still. He was not as unbending as the iron he forged, though at this moment his *schwanz* felt as if it had been held over a red-hot fire. He'd not been with a woman since Nina. His body was tense. One hand made circles on Lottie's back and the other rested on her hip, holding her to him.

He thought she'd fallen asleep, when her fingers

gently stroked the side of his chin. That soft touch caused his hand to dig into her hip.

Her head came up, and she peered into his eyes. Their color had darkened. He saw yearning in the depths of those jade pools.

She moved first, pressing her lips to his, her body to his.

He grasped her hips, pulling her onto his lap, straddling her legs on either side of his thighs.

Her body covered his. Her lips moved over his as if she were feasting on a sweet.

To keep his hands away from intimate places on her body, he cradled her head in his hands and kept his mind on kissing rather than the way her body swayed on his lap, seating her hot center over his appendage that ached.

The horse snorted.

He drew out of the kiss. "We need to go."

Her eyes were glazed with desire as she peered at him. "Why?"

"Because I can no longer keep my mind off anything other than touching you where I shouldn't."

Slowly, her dazed eyes cleared and glistened with heat. "I wish you to touch me in all the places that have come to life."

Manfred shook his head. "That will only happen when we are hidden away in our bedroom as man and wife."

Her face lit up. "Man and wife? You wish to marry me?"

Grinning, he nodded and kissed her delightful nose. "Ja. The sooner, the better."

She hugged him. "I feel the same way."

"I'll ask Beau for your hand when we return." Manfred placed his hands on Lottie's waist, raising her to her feet.

She stood, straddling his legs and peering down at him.

He'd never wanted a woman, not even Nina, as much as he wanted this woman. She would be strong enough to work with him and to bear him children and to love him all night long.

Lottie stepped to the side, allowing him to rise. She held out her hand to help him up.

He grasped her hand, using his legs to push him up rather than her pulling on him.

When he stood, he kept their hands clasped as they walked back to the buggy. He was thankful the horse had stayed. In his rush to catch up to Lottie, he'd not tethered the animal.

"Church is over now." Lottie said it as if she were a child in trouble.

"We'll go to the boarding house. If anyone noticed we weren't at services, we'll just tell them we were talking about our future." He placed his hands around her waist and lifted her into the buggy.

She placed her hands on his before he removed them from her waist. "I don't care about talk as long as I have your trust."
Staring into her eyes, he saw more than trust. He liked what he saw.

Chapter Fifteen

Lottie Mae knew it was silly to feel so happy and worried at the same time. She was happy that Manfred believed her about how she came to be soiled and worried that someone would come along and ruin this bit of happiness that had come into her life.

He stopped the horse and buggy in front of the boarding house and hopped out before raising his arms to help her down.

She dropped into his hands, smiling. He would never hurt her or allow her to be hurt.

Manfred placed her on the ground with space between them. "Do you want me to go in with you or return the buggy and come along after?"

Lottie Mae understood he was giving her time to tell the others where she had been before he came calling. However, she'd rather he be by her side as she entered the house. "Come in with me, please."

He nodded, tied the horse to the hitching rail, and placed her hand through the crook of his arm.

The smile tugging at the corners of her mouth couldn't be dimmed. Manfred believed in her and had asked her to be his wife.

Freedom opened the door as they stepped onto the porch. "Where have you two been?" she asked, her smile broad and eyes filled with merriment.

Lottie Mae glanced back at the buggy. "We went for a buggy ride when the park was full of people." She didn't think about how that sounded until Freedom's eyebrows raised.

"We wanted a quiet place to talk things over," Manfred said, speaking up, escorting her through the door, and into the parlor.

Everyone, including Jules and Beau, sat or stood in the parlor.

Beau came to his feet. "Where have you two been?"

The glower on his face would have made her shrink away, if not for Manfred squeezing her hand against his body with his arm.

"We went for a buggy ride to discuss Lottie's past and our future." Manfred led her over to the chair Beau had vacated. He made sure she was settled before shifting his attention to Beau. "I would like your approval to marry Lottie."

Beau glanced over at her. "Is this what you want?"

She nodded. "It is."

"Then I won't stand in the way." Beau grabbed Manfred's hand and shook. Jules moved toward the men and the women swarmed Lottie Mae.

"That's wonderful!" exclaimed Freedom. Belle patted her shoulder but didn't look as sure of the marriage. Liesa hugged her, and Mrs. Dearling nearly squeezed all the air out of her. Darie sat on the chair in the corner, stitching.

"When are you getting married?" Freedom asked.

Lottie Mae caught Manfred's gaze. "We haven't decided, but soon."

He smiled, and heat crept into her cheeks.

"You can wear the dress Savannah gave you for the dance," Liesa said.

For half an hour everyone talked at once, making it hard for her to talk with Manfred or Darie. The more plans were made, the more it seemed as if Darie was dissolving into the chair. Something was bothering her.

"Landsakes! Dinner will be cold. Come on, everyone, let's eat," Mrs. Dearling said, waving everyone out of the parlor.

"You go ahead," Lottie Mae said, motioning for Manfred to go as well. She put a hand on Darie's shoulder, keeping her in the room.

Manfred nodded and ushered the last person down the hall to the kitchen.

"Why do you look so sad?" Lottie Mae asked the young woman.

"When you marry and move, no one will understand." She didn't glance up from her handiwork.

"Everyone here understands. Who do you think helped me?"

She shook her head. "It's not the same. We know who did it. He knows where we are."

"But if I'm married and living away from the boarding house, he has no reason to know you live here." She'd thought about this as she and Manfred talked on the way back from the spring. If Thomas came after her, she would be with Manfred. He would protect her, and it would keep Thomas from finding Darie. She feared more for the young woman, who didn't have a strong man—well she had Beau—but not all the time, like she would have Manfred.

"He'll find out. I know he will."

The fear on Darie's face made Lottie Mae's heart ache. She'd been as scared as Darie when Beau came along and coaxed her into his wagon and to Shady Gulch. "Everyone in this boarding house and town will help you. Many people owe Beau. They'll all keep an eye out and let him know when Thomas comes to town." She plucked the needlework from Darie's hands. "Come on. You need to eat."

The two walked down the hall and into the kitchen and the middle of a conversation about her wedding.

Manfred understood that even though he and Lottie were getting married, Mrs. Dearling had rules in her house. But he'd had a horrible time not kissing Lottie good night as he left the boarding house. After the kisses they'd shared at the spring, he had a hankering for more.

It looked like he better head to the bathhouse and slip into a cold tub of water to alleviate his heated body.

"Manfred, didn't see you or Lottie Mae at church services," Reverend Webster said, falling in step beside him.

He grinned. There would be many who insinuated the same thing. It would be best to get the information to the man who could spread the good news and keep it from becoming unfavorable. "Me and Lottie went for a buggy ride to discuss our future. Too many people at the boarding house, too many people in the park, and asking her into my shop would start rumors." He continued walking.

"That's good news!" The reverend slapped him on the back. "Will I be performing the ceremony?"

Manfred spun toward him. "Why wouldn't you?"

"I know that most of your countrymen are Lutheran."

He waved a hand. "God is God if you are in a church. And Lottie would be happy to see you performing the ceremony."

"When will this ceremony be? I'm sure my wife would like to offer a dress for the occasion."

"*Nien,* there was talk of Lottie wearing the dress from the recent social."

"If that's what she wants, I'll let Savannah know." Reverend Webster touched his hat and headed down the street.

Manfred wondered how many times he'd have to explain why he and Lottie hadn't been at the services today.

At the bath house, Jin Yung, the owner, bowed. "Mr. Big Man, this not your night to take bath."

Manfred had tried to get the small Chinaman to call him by his name, but he insisted he was Big Man. "I would like cold water in a bath tonight. It was a warm day." He walked into the room with the large tub. He'd built the tub himself when he'd realized the Chinaman didn't have one in which he could sit and soak.

"You no work today. It your church day." The little man kept up the banter as he filled the tub and Manfred stripped.

He'd learned after the third time he'd bathed here, that Mr. Yung didn't really expect answers, he just talked.

"Stranger here earlier. Him look dirty, like he been riding horse long time. When I asked, he told me hold my tongue or he'd take it from my head." Mr. Yung shook his head. "Not a nice man."

This caught Manfred's attention. "What did he look like?"

"Tall."

All men were tall to the Chinaman.

"Light hair, crooked nose."

Manfred stood up out of the water, splashing it all over the dirt floor. "I have to go. If that man comes back, send someone to get me." He was redressed and striding down the street to the saloon in minutes.

He pounded on the front doors of the Silver Dollar Saloon. Beau closed the bar on Sundays. But he lived upstairs.

"Beau! Open the door!" he shouted.

"What the He—!" Beau jerked the door open and stared at Manfred. "What did you do, change your mind and can't face Lottie Mae alone?"

"No. Mr. Yung said a man who looked like that bastard who hurt Lottie and Darie was in the bath house tonight."

"Damn!" Beau opened the door farther. He wore only his pants. "Wait here. I'll get dressed and tell Jules to watch the boarding house. We'll go get our sheriff to do his job."

Chapter Sixteen

Lottie Mae was so happy, she couldn't fall asleep. It had been years since her heart sang with happiness. She was getting married. She would have children and a wonderful life. So many nights she'd lain awake, angry with herself and all that had happened to her.

The sound of someone moving in the room next door caught her attention. Why would Darie be up at this late hour?

She slipped out of bed and padded across the room to the door. Opening the door, she caught a glimpse of Darie in day clothes going down the stairs.

Lottie Mae hurried down the hallway and thudded down the stairs in her haste to catch the young woman. There was only one reason she would be fully dressed and sneaking out of the house. She planned to leave town. It was the worst thing she could do. Here she would be protected.

One step out the door, she spotted Darie on the street.

"Darie! Wait!" she called out as a man slipped out of the darkness and took Darie by the arm.

"No! Leave her alone!" Lottie Mae ran out into the street, throwing her body into the man.

"*Merde*!" A familiar curse floated on the night air.

She stepped back as Jules picked up the fighting Darie. "She must go back to the house." Jules said, in his Cajun accent.

"Yes. I heard her moving about." She put a hand on Darie, trying to calm the woman. "Darie, it's Jules. Stop struggling."

They managed to get the woman with flailing arms and legs through the back door and into the parlor. Jules placed her on the settee.

"You cannot leave this house. The man you fear is in town. That is why I was watching." Jules stared down a Darie. While his eyes held concern, his face had a stern frown.

Lottie Mae dropped to the settee beside Darie. "You have to believe this is the safest place for you to be."

Darie shook her head. "There is nowhere safe."

"Then why were you leaving?" She didn't understand this young woman's thinking.

The smaller woman dropped her chin to her chest. "To keep you safe."

The sacrifice Darie had tried to make, humbled and angered her. "You don't need to keep me safe. I have Manfred, Beau, and Jules." She smiled at the dark-skinned man staring down at Darie as if she would spring off the settee and dart out the door. "And you do, too."

"Beau and your man told Sheriff Blake the stranger is back. The three are looking for the coward," Jules said.

Lottie Mae put her arm around Darie and helped her stand. "Come on. The safest place for both of us is here, in this boarding house, with so many people keeping watch over us." She led the woman to the door and glanced over her shoulder at Jules. "Thank you."

He nodded.

She continued up the stairs with Darie, helping her to undress and get into bed.

"I'll sit right here in this chair until you fall asleep. Thomas isn't going to hurt you again. We will all see to that." Lottie Mae settled onto the hard chair and waited until Darie was breathing slow and even before sneaking out the door and into her room.

Having Darie think she could lure Thomas away and save her was endearing but foolish. Once Thomas had his way with Darie and perhaps killed her, he'd come back for her. The only way either of them would be safe was if he were in jail for good or dead.

Manfred met Beau and Sheriff Blake back at the Sheriff's Office after they all scoured the town looking for the stranger.

"No one I talked to has seen him," Beau said, frustration making his words come out on a growl.

"You're sure he's here?" Sheriff Blake asked.

"Jin Yung wouldn't have made it up. He doesn't know we want this man out of town," Manfred said. "Maybe he's hanging around the boarding house." The thought lodged in his mind like a burr on a piece of forged iron.

"Jules will bring him here." Beau glanced at his pocket watch. "It's three in the morning. We all have work tomorrow. I'll relieve Jules."

Manfred walked out of the office with Beau. "I can help watch the boarding house."

"If we don't catch that bastard by tomorrow night, you can have a shift." Beau strode down the street toward the boarding house.

Manfred fell in step beside him. It was on his way to his place. "I think I should marry Lottie soon. That way she will be with me all the time."

"It's not a bad idea, but then, we'd have to keep an eye on two places. It's better if you wait until this guy is caught."

"Or dead," Manfred said.

Beau stopped and put a hand on his chest. "You can't kill this guy even though it's what he deserves."

"If he threatens Lottie, he will get what is coming to him." Manfred had already made his peace with the fact that if the stranger hurt Lottie, he would do what was necessary to keep it from happening again.

"You can't take the law into your own hands."

"I have the right to protect my family. Lottie will soon be my wife." He flexed his hands.

"She won't have a family if you get put in jail for killing the man." Beau took off again.

Manfred nodded his head. He would only hurt the man if he hurt Lottie.

They came upon Jules in the alley between the saloon and the boarding house.

"We can't find the bastard," Beau said.

"Darie tried to run. Lottie Mae and I stopped her." Jules scanned the alley. "Thought I saw someone at the end of the alley when Darie was kicking and swinging her arms to get free." He scratched the side of his cheek. "I look when I come out. I see nothing."

"What about Lottie? Where is she?" Manfred stepped in front of Jules. The man's strange accent and the way he talked, made it hard for Manfred to understand everything he said.

"She is fine. Calmed the little one down."

"I'll take over for now. Ty will send a deputy to keep an eye on things when it's light." Beau patted Jules on the back. "Get some sleep."

The other man headed to the back of the saloon.

"You too. You won't be any good if you don't get some sleep." Beau waved a hand in the direction of the blacksmith shop.

Manfred didn't want to leave the boarding house but wanted to be ready to help the next night if he was needed. Walking along the side of the building, he peered up at what he thought might be Lottie's room. "Sleep well," he whispered.

His feet grew heavier as he neared his place. Even though he was worried about Lottie, he knew Beau wouldn't let anything happen to her. He passed the hardware store and caught a flicker of light through the window of his blacksmith shop. His groggy mind came awake at the sight. He strode forward, forgetting his tiredness.

Manfred yanked open the big door to his shop and spotted a small fire in the corner. He picked up a shovel and tossed dirt from the floor onto the flames. Who would want to set fire to his business? His home? Had the person hoped he was sleeping? The more he thought about it, the angrier he became.

He stomped the last of the embers out and swore in German. The fire had just been started. That meant the culprit had to be close by. Had he scared the person with his approach?

Now that the flames were out, the shop was dark. He fumbled his way to the door. He'd report this to Sheriff Blake. Using the half-moon's light, he made his way to Depot Street and the Sheriff's Office.

"What are you doing back here?" Sheriff Blake asked, swinging his booted feet off his desk and onto the floor.

"Someone just tried to burn down my place."

"What are you talking about?" The sheriff shot to his feet.

Manfred told him about returning to his shop and what he found and did.

"I want to see this." Sheriff Blake plucked the lantern, hanging from a hook in the ceiling, and strode to the door. "Come on. I need to see the damage and decide if it's safe for you to stay there."

"I will stay in my shop." No one was going to scare him away from his business.

"We'll see about it."

The sun coated Shady Gulch with a golden glow by the time Sheriff Blake had searched the remains of the fire, the shop, and fetched the deputy to take over for Beau and send the saloon owner to Manfred's blacksmith shop.

"Manfred, are you hurt?" Beau asked, jogging up

to the building.

"I am fine. I just need sleep." He'd been leaning against the building as the sheriff did a look about the outside of his shop.

"Did Ty say you couldn't go in and sleep?" Beau opened the shop door and motioned for him to go in.

"He's checking outside my shop. Something about impressions." Manfred started into the building and spun back around. "Don't tell Lottie. I don't want her to worry."

Beau raised an eyebrow. "You don't think the first person who comes in the saloon today won't be talking about this?"

He nodded. Rumors and truth seemed to pour into the saloon like the whiskey and beer poured into the glasses.

Manfred shrugged and entered his shop, walked through, not looking at the charred wood in the corner, and headed straight for his cot. Unlike Beau, who ran an establishment that stayed open until the early morning hours, he was used to being asleep by nine and up by six. Instead he'd missed a night's sleep and was going to bed when he usually rose.

He untied his boots and dropped them on the floor beside his bed. He dreamed he was climbing in beside Lottie and drifted off.

Pounding woke him. Manfred dug fists into his scratchy eyes before pulling his pocket watch out of his trouser pocket and snapping it open.

Eight.

He'd had two hours of sleep.

"Mr. Albrecht, wake up! You sick?" A young male

voice called.

"One minute!" he hollered back and shoved his body off the cot. He'd help whoever was out there and then put up a sign saying he was gone. He needed to sleep. He had to be rested to help watch the boarding house tonight.

His hands dug into the water in his basin and splashed his face. Drying his face, the toweling caught on his whisker stubble. While he couldn't help getting dirty from his work, he never looked unkempt. The man staring back at him in the mirror looked like the man he'd seen the month after he'd lost his family. That wasn't going to happen again.

"Mr. Albrecht!" The pounding started again.

He growled, pulled on his boots, and tied them.

"Coming!" He stormed through the shop and opened the door. Joshua Montgomery, the liveryman's son, backed away from the door.

"What was so important?" Manfred asked, in a tone angrier than he'd meant.

The boy took another step back. "Beau told me to keep an eye out for the man the sheriff had locked up a couple days ago. He's here. Seen him sneakin' around inside the livery early this mornin'."

"Why didn't you tell Beau?"

"Couldn't find 'im. And he told me to tell you if I couldn't." The boy spun on his heels and ran down the street to the livery and stockyards.

There went his few hours of sleep this morning. Had the boy only looked at the saloon to find Beau? If so, he could have told Jules, or the man's partner would have told the boy where to find Beau. He didn't like this. Not one little bit.

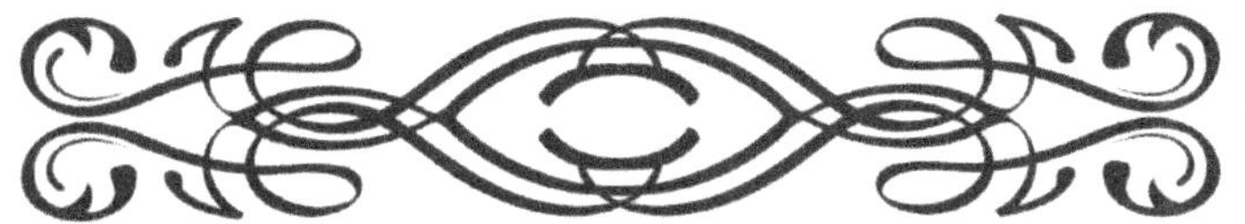

Chapter Seventeen

Her curtains rustled in the early morning breeze. Lottie Mae sat up and stretched. Even for all that had happened the night before, she'd slept well.

"Beau? Beau?"

Manfred's voice calling to Beau launched her from the bed and to the window. The man she'd dreamed about all night stood in the alley between the saloon and boarding house looking all around.

She pushed the window up higher and leaned out. "What's wrong?"

Manfred's head snapped side to side, before he glanced up. "Stay inside. I will come to you."

Lottie Mae nodded and drew her upper body back into the room. Manfred was coming to see her. She needed to dress.

It was hours until she had to work in the saloon. She dropped her nightgown, pulled on a shift and drawers, and stepped into an everyday dress. She'd worry about a corset and other undergarments later. She just needed to be covered to receive Manfred in the parlor. She slipped her feet into slippers and hurried down the stairs, brushing her hair.

A soft rap on the door as she stepped off the bottom stair had her running for the front door. She swung the door open.

Manfred stood there looking disheveled and manly.

"Come in," she said, as he stared, making no effort to step over the threshold. "Come on." She grasped his arm, drawing him in, and closing the door.

"Why are you looking for Beau?"

He reached out, capturing a handful of her hair. "Your hair is a beautiful color. And it's so soft."

Her heart fluttered, and her cheeks warmed at his compliment. "Thank you. But why were you looking for Beau in the alley?"

"Who are you talking to?" Mrs. Dearling asked, walking into the parlor. "Landsakes! What are you two doing?" She stepped between them. "Lottie Mae, get your hair up. Manfred, why did you come calling without dressing proper?"

"I need to find Beau," Manfred said, his gaze remaining on Lottie Mae.

"He's in the kitchen having coffee and toast." Mrs. Dearling wrapped an arm around his and dragged him from the room. "Come along. Lottie Mae, go get presentable."

Not wanting to miss any of the conversation between Manfred and Beau, Lottie Mae wound her hair on her head and stabbed a pencil from the writing desk through the bun. She walked to the kitchen and stood inside the door, her arms crossed over her chest, so no one would be the wiser she hadn't put a corset on.

"Joshua Montgomery said he couldn't find you to tell you the man we're watching for was lurking around in the livery this morning." Manfred had sat down across the table from Beau. They both had a cup of coffee in their hands.

"He had to be the one who started the fire in your shop—"

"What fire? Where?" Lottie Mae forgot she was going to stand back and listen when Beau mentioned a fire in Manfred's shop. She rushed over to Manfred and grasped his head. "Were you hurt? Why didn't you tell me?"

Manfred gathered her into his arms and sat her on his lap. "I am fine, *schatzi*. I was not at the shop when it was started and arrived soon enough to put it out."

"All of this is because of me." Her heart ached for the big man.

"We do not know it is because of you. Maybe I made a person mad and they do this."

She knew he only said it to make her feel better. It didn't help.

Beau cleared his throat. They both looked at him. "It would be a good idea if you and Darie stay inside the boarding house until we catch this Decker."

"You need me in the saloon. He would be stupid to try anything in there." She wasn't going to allow Thomas to make her lose this job.

"She is safer in the saloon than here," Manfred said.

She smiled at him and leaned against his chest.

"What about Darie? It took a lot of convincing last night to keep her from running off. She says if she leaves, I'll be safe. But I won't. We have to stay together."

"She should also be in the saloon," Manfred added.

"She wouldn't be able to take sitting in the room with that many men." Lottie Mae peered into Manfred's face. "It was a long time before I could even stand a man looking at me, let alone talking to me and being in the same room."

"I'll take her up to my rooms over the saloon before we open." Beau sipped his coffee.

"What is she going to do up there for the hours the saloon is open?" she asked, enjoying Manfred's warmth and closeness.

"I can go up with her. We can work on our stitching," Mrs. Dearling said, turning from the stove and narrowing her eyes at Lottie Mae.

She knew the older woman didn't approve of her sitting on Manfred's lap, but she liked it. Manfred's hand on her leg under the table gave her a conspiratorial squeeze.

"We can find something to eat when we come over for meals," she added.

Beau shook his head. "I'll get Savannah to sit with Darie upstairs. Mrs. Dearling can make the meals. You ladies can eat them upstairs to break up the boredom for Savannah and Darie."

"What will the men think, seeing us traipsing up and down the stairs?" Lottie Mae didn't want any of them thinking the saloon had changed its stand on how the women were treated.

"If Darie and Savannah are already up there before

we open, and Mrs. Dearling brings dinner over and the first two to take their dinner can help carry it upstairs, no one will think anything of you taking your regular mealtime upstairs. Jules and I will eat, as usual, in the saloon." Beau stood. "I'll go tell Savannah we need her help and clue Jules in."

He left the kitchen through the back door.

Mrs. Dearling glared at her and Manfred before returning her attention to the pot on the stove.

Lottie Mae grinned at Manfred and rubbed her hand over the stubble of whiskers. "You're sure you weren't hurt in the fire?"

He turned his head and kissed her knuckles. "I am fine. Only tired." His arm slid around her waist, pulling her tighter against him as he leaned his head on her shoulder.

"You can't sleep in my kitchen." Mrs. Dearling walked over to them waving a spoon.

Manfred raised his head, grinned at Lottie Mae, and released her.

She stood and Manfred rose.

"I will go back to my shop, put up a sign I am gone, and will sleep."

She didn't like the idea of him being disturbed. Even worse, if it had been Thomas who started the fire, there was nothing to keep him from returning and trying something else. "Why don't you lie down on the settee and sleep. No one here will disturb you." She glanced at Mrs. Dearling to get the older woman to agree.

"He'll never fit comfortably on that piece of furniture," the woman huffed. "If you want peace and quiet, this is the place." She put her spoon down and waved a hand. "Follow me."

Lottie Mae was surprised the older woman had given in so easily. Would she put Manfred where she could sneak in and share a kiss or two?

No. They weren't that lucky. Mrs. Dearling offered Manfred her bed in the small room off the kitchen. The only way in or out was through the kitchen. She'd be keeping watch that Lottie Mae didn't steal in for some private time with her betrothed.

Lottie Mae had to convince Darie she would be safer in Beau's quarters over the saloon than in the boarding house with Mrs. Dearling. Once the girl had agreed, they packed up her needlework and walked across the alley and into the back of the saloon.

"It stinks in here," Darie said, pinching her nose with her free hand.

"You get used to it." Lottie Mae inhaled deep and realized it wasn't the most pleasant of odors, but she had gotten used to the smell of stale cigar smoke, spilled beer, and unwashed men.

Beau stood behind the bar. "Do you know which room is mine?"

"The one on the left?" she ventured, having only witnessed him walking in the room a couple of times during business hours.

He nodded. "I cleaned it up. If you want to open the window that's fine, but don't stand in front of it or hang out. Don't want people thinking I keep one of you girls in my room." He winked but she felt Darie stiffen.

"It's alright. He's joking," she said, while silently knowing he was making sure no one, he or a woman from his establishment, were talked about negatively.

She was curious to see what Beau's room looked like. No one other than Jules and Mrs. Dearling, who came up and cleaned and gathered the sheets, had been allowed in his room until today.

At the top of the stairs, they walked to the left and stopped in front of the only door. She opened it and immediately knew it was Beau's. He had a distinctive scent that was all his own. It had a hint of spice with a bit of swarthiness she'd not smelled on any other man.

The room was tidy and had massive, well-made furniture. A large bed and bureau of a dark wood sat along one wall. A wardrobe and tables on either side of the bed were of the same dark wood. The room was large enough two stuffed chairs and a low table between them with a kerosene lamp made a small sitting area in one corner. A picture of a beautiful woman sat on the bureau. She had dark hair and a picture smile that didn't light up her eyes. Her fancy clothing and unhappy expression made Lottie Mae wonder if this woman was the reason Beau had ended up in Shady Gulch and befriended women in need.

A narrow door in the opposite corner drew her attention. Darie appeared just as intrigued as Lottie Mae. The younger woman followed her across the room to the door.

Lottie Mae opened it and discovered a small room with a wash basin and commode. "You won't have to worry about going down to the outhouse," she said, showing Darie the interior of the small room.

The young woman's cheeks darkened in color.

"Find a comfy chair. I'll stay until Savannah

arrives." Lottie Mae sat in the seat closest to the door and picked up a book that sat on the table between the chairs. She smiled. It was Jules Verne's *Twenty Thousand Leagues under the Sea*. She'd enjoyed reading this to her class. Opening the book to the paper Beau must have used to mark his place, she began reading.

"What are you reading?" Darie asked.

She held up the book, allowing the young woman to read the title.

"That is a good book. Our teacher read it to us and it was to be read by the students where I was headed to teach." At the mention of not continuing to her destination, Darie's shoulders slumped.

"You'll feel up to teaching again one day." She read a line in the book and remembered the students' spellbound attention. "I'm ready to try it again."

The click of a woman's boots on the boards outside the door stopped. The door swung open and Savannah entered, her arms full of a beautiful green cloth. She smiled at Lottie Mae and Darie. "Seein's how Mrs. Dearling told me Miss Darie is somethang special with a needle and thread, she and I are goin' to make a weddin' dress."

Darie's eyes lit up.

Lottie Mae's mouth dropped open. She snapped it shut before saying, "You don't have to do that for me. I planned to use the beautiful dress you gave me for the dance."

"Nonsense. Beau told me to purchase fabric and make a dress. That's what me," she glanced over at Darie and winked, "and Darie will do while we wait for that consarned man to show his face and be chunked in jail."

The fabric was a beautiful green the color of spring grass. It was soft and flowed as Savannah draped it over Lottie Mae's shoulders as she and Darie discussed the style of the garment.

"Fetch her measurements and I'll make sure the floor is clean enough to lay the fabric down to cut." Savannah vanished into the wash room.

"Make sure she doesn't make anything too fancy." Lottie Mae said to Darie as the younger woman used a tape measure to check her measurements and write them down. She wore her saloon dress, which made the measurements more accurate due to the tight fit of the garment at her waist and the short puffy sleeves didn't get in the way when she measured for arm length.

Savannah had rolled up the rug by the bed and washed the floor by the time Darie said Lottie Mae could leave.

"I'll be thinking about what you two are doing up here while I'm at work," Lottie Mae said, stopping in the open door.

"Ya'll are goin' to be happy as a kitten in milk when you see this." Savannah waved her out of the room as Darie placed the fabric on the floor.

Lottie Mae slipped out of the room and sauntered down the stairs.

Beau, Jules, Ty, Lark, and Manfred all sat at a table, their heads bowed toward the center, talking low.

"What are you talking about?" she asked, walking up behind Manfred.

Chapter Eighteen

Manfred had heard someone come down the stairs but hadn't expected it to be Lottie. He put a hand behind him, hoping she'd grasp it.

She did. He pulled her beside him. Everyone, except he and the reverend, thought the women shouldn't know about the stranger. He wanted to make sure Lottie knew everything. That way she would be more likely to listen to what they had to say and not do something that would put her in danger.

"The man is here," he said.

"I know. That's why Darie is upstairs. To keep her safe." Lottie gazed into his eyes as if she were searching for something.

"He's hiding pretty good," Sheriff Blake said, drawing their attention. "We," he indicated Beau, Jules, Manfred, the reverend, and himself, "looked for him most of the night and didn't find him. But Joshua saw him in the livery. Makes us think he's going to sleep there tonight."

Manfred nodded. They would catch the man tonight. He was sure of it. As long as the two women stayed in the saloon, they'd be safe.

"Do you plan to catch him there?" Lottie Mae asked.

"Ja," he answered. "We will make sure he no longer comes to this town."

Lottie gasped. "You aren't going to—to kill him?" Her gaze swept around the table, landing on the reverend.

"We won't kill him. Just persuade him he isn't wanted in this town."

Manfred studied the preacher. He'd heard rumors the man had been on the other side of the law before arriving in Shady Gulch.

"We won't do anything illegal. But this man doesn't seem to listen when he's told to stay away," Sheriff Blake said.

Manfred nodded. "He will know we mean business when we catch him tonight."

Lottie released his hand and backed away from the table. "Don't be as cruel as he is."

He'd thought she'd be happy to learn the man would be sent out of town with his tail between his legs.

A foot kicked his under the table. Manfred glanced at Beau. The saloon owner nodded for him to follow Lottie. She'd disappeared into the back room.

Unsure what to say, he shoved the chair back and walked into the dark room. He found Lottie sitting on a barrel, her arms wrapped around herself.

"What bothers you, *schatzi*?" he asked, walking up

to her and drawing her into his arms. Holding her, inhaling her scent, he never wanted anything bad to happen to her again.

She spun in his arms, burying her face into his shirt. "I don't want to lose you, or Beau, or Jules." She wiped her nose on his shirt and raised her face.

He couldn't see what she was feeling due to the dimness in the room. "You won't lose us. We will be careful."

"It's not just to the law." She put her hands on either side of his face. "It's to lawlessness. If you beat him up as he beat up me and Darie, you are no better than he is. Have Ty put him in jail and I'll bring charges against him. I don't care if it ruins my chances to teach, I'll have you."

He held her tight. If she told her story to a judge, the whole town would know her past. That she was willing to do this to keep others safe, humbled him. He also didn't want her to have to face the scorn of so many who would be like her parents and the town where she left.

"You are brave. Braver than me. I do not wish you to go through that pain again." He kissed the top of her head.

"Darie will tell her story. They'll have to believe two of us." She continued to hold his head.

He could see she tried as hard as he did to see into one another's eyes.

"Are you sure Darie will talk?" He found it hard to believe the young woman had the courage to voice her humiliation to a judge and a jury of all men.

When she didn't answer right away, he leaned down, pressing his lips to hers. She grasped his hair in her hands and held his mouth to hers as if their melded lips were her anchor. He didn't mind the lingering kiss. He'd been dreaming of a kiss that wasn't quite so desperate as he slept in the house with Lottie so close.

Her body relaxed, and her fingers loosened their grip on his hair. He tipped his head, capturing her mouth differently, guiding her lips apart, and deepening the kiss with his tongue.

She moaned and pressed her body closer.

Once she realized he would only make her body happy and not hurt her, she would be a voracious lover.

Female voices and the backdoor opening, had him ripping his lips from hers and putting space between them.

Lottie grabbed his shirt, drawing him deeper into a corner where they were hidden behind stacked barrels of beer.

He grinned and pulled her back into his arms as the voices and footsteps moved on by.

"You have rekindled my heart," he whispered in her ear and nibbled on her neck.

She sighed, dropping her head to the side, allowing him more of her neck to kiss.

"What do you mean Lottie Mae and Manfred aren't in the backroom?" Beau said loudly.

Manfred had forgotten the men knew they were in this room. "I hope I didn't make you too disheveled," he whispered, kissing her on the lips. "I'll go out the back after you present yourself."

"Why can't we go in together?" Lottie asked.

He grasped her hand, placing it on his throbbing *schwanz*. "This is why we cannot walk out together.

They will know, we have been *küssen.*"

He'd expected her to pull her hand back, but she held it there as if curious and testing her own resolve.

"Lottie Mae?" Beau called.

"You must go," Manfred whispered and gave her a push away from him. He followed her dark shadow as she walked toward the light of the saloon where Beau held the blanket to the side.

He waited for the blanket to close before making his way to the backdoor and out into the alley. He leaned against the back wall until his *schwanz* no longer made walking painful. After that, he wasn't sure he could follow Beau's advice and wait to get married until after the stranger was no longer a threat.

Lottie Mae knew her cheeks were red because they burned as if she'd been out in a freezing wind. Beau raised an eyebrow at the sight of her. Ty and Lark were gone, but there were a couple of patrons at a table. The other ladies stood at the bar watching her entrance.

"Was Manfred back there with you?" Belle asked, her foot tapping like an irritated mother.

"He was." She didn't want to lie, but she didn't want the men at the table to hear this discussion. "I don't want to talk about it." She marched behind the bar and picked up a towel to wipe the wood top.

Freedom pointed to her hair. "You might want to fix that."

She spun to the mirror behind the bar and stared in shock at the tendrils trailing down from her lopsided bun. She had no recollection of Manfred putting his hands on her head, but she looked as if she'd been in a wind storm or…she glanced at her red puffy lips…thoroughly kissed.

Lottie Mae pushed past Beau and charged up the stairs to the room where Savannah and Darie were working on her dress. She needed privacy to check her hair and didn't want to chance running into Manfred if she went to the boarding house.

Several people burst out in laughter as she climbed the stairs and stepped through the door, closing out the laughter.

Savannah and Darie both looked up from where they knelt on the floor next to the fabric.

"What happened to you?" Savannah asked, rising to her feet.

"Nothing." She strode to the wash room, opened the door, stepped in, and closed the door.

There was a small window that allowed light to filter in. She used the light and mirror to fix her hair. She poured water from a pitcher into the bowl and dabbed the tepid water on her lips, trying to reduce the puffiness.

Her swollen lips reminded her of where Manfred had placed her hand. Her cheeks heated at the thought. That part of him had felt alive as she'd held her hand still. It had surged and hardened even as her hand had lingered. She'd witnessed little of what had happened to her when the three had attacked. One had held her skirts over her head as they violated her. But she knew from animals on the farm and bits and pieces she'd picked up from women who'd been at the boarding house, that when a man swelled like that it meant he desired the female.

"Are you sure y'all are alright?" Savannah asked,

opening the door.

She'd met Savannah before she became the preacher's wife. Savannah was of a higher social status than Lottie Mae but once she'd realized status didn't mean much in Shady Gulch, Savannah had shown she was as down to earth as the rest of them.

Lottie Mae grabbed Savannah by the arm and pulled her into the small room, closing the door. They stood close together.

"What's wrong with you?" Savannah asked, putting a hand to Lottie Mae's forehead.

"Nothing marrying Manfred won't cure." She raised an eyebrow.

The other woman grinned. "Y'all were gettin' sugar and it messed up your hair."

She nodded. "I made him swell."

Savannah tried to take a step back and ran into the door. "Don't go tellin' Beau that or he'll get tetchy. Why are you tellin' me?"

"You're a married woman. Will his swelling like that be bad for him? Because he can't…do anything until we're married?" She didn't want to cause Manfred pain. If that were the case, she'd have to stay away from him until they were man and wife.

"Cold water takes the swellin' down. You best get back down to the saloon. I don't want Beau bargin' up here and scarin' Darie."

Lottie Mae nodded and opened the door, allowing Savannah to exit first. She had her answer and her hair was back in place. With a newfound composure, she walked down the stairs and noted the room was a third full. Why did there have to be so many thirsty men in this town?

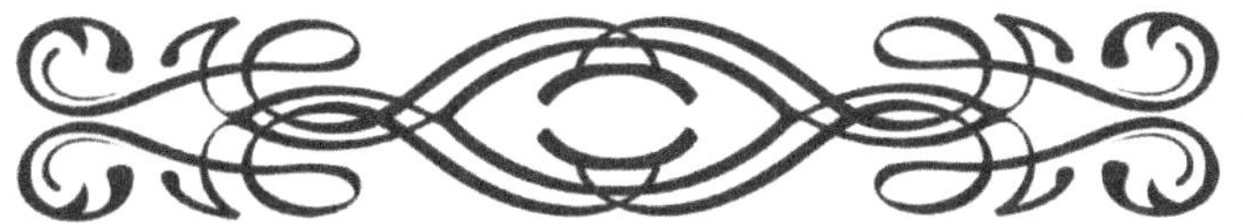

Chapter Nineteen

Mrs. Dearling brought dinner over to the saloon as planned. Lottie Mae and Freedom helped carry it to the room upstairs. The patrons' gazes followed them as they ascended even though Mrs. Dearling followed them.

Lottie Mae placed the tray on the table in the room and closed the door behind Mrs. Dearling.

"Darie and I were just wonderin' when some food would arrive. We've worked up an appetite sewin'." Savannah pulled the towel off the tray and inhaled.

Lottie Mae's stomach grumbled at the scent of pork, bread, and green beans. She picked up a plate and sat on the bed.

Savannah took a spot beside her while Darie plopped on the floor and Freedom and Mrs. Dearling sat in the chairs.

"It feels good to get off my feet," Freedom said,

lifting a forkful of beans to her mouth.

"I noticed Jules has been playing a lot of dance songs," Savannah said. She'd know which songs were played for dancing and which for entertainment, having worked in the saloon before marrying Lark.

"If he keeps playing songs we dance to instead of ones I sing to, I don't think my legs and feet can take much more. There are too many men down there today to keep dancing and carrying trays." Freedom frowned. It was an expression rarely seen on her face.

"I'd come help but Beau told me to stay behind the bar. I think he thinks—" Lottie Mae stopped, when Darie's eyes widened and she put her fork down.

Savannah nudged Lottie Mae with an elbow and glared.

Mrs. Dearling picked up the conversation, telling about her trip to the mercantile and who she visited with.

Lottie Mae finished her meal first and excused herself. She didn't want to open her mouth and say something else that would upset Darie.

She descended the stairs and spotted Manfred standing at his usual place at the end of the bar. He'd cleaned up, shaved, and was wearing a clean shirt and trousers. If she didn't know better, she'd think he came here to impress someone. A smile curved her lips as she stepped behind the bar and slowly worked her way down to where he stood.

"You look fancy tonight," she said softly, so the man only a few feet away couldn't hear.

"I have my eye on a woman. I want to impress her." Manfred winked and raised his mug of beer.

Lottie Mae laughed and went to work filling

glasses at the bar and thinking about her encounter in the back room with the man watching her every move.

Liesa and Belle went upstairs when Freedom came down. Seeing her friend, reminded Lottie Mae to say something to Beau about Freedom and the others having to dance so much today.

She sauntered down the bar and stood beside Beau. "You need to ask Jules to not play any more dance songs. Freedom said her feet and legs are about to give out."

He shrugged. "I'll mention it to Jules, but I think he's been taking requests."

"Requests? From who?" She scanned the room and only spotted the regulars with a couple of new faces at one of the card tables. Pushing by Beau to the end of the bar near the back room, she had a better look at the faces of the two playing cards. Her heart lodged in her throat. Billy and Delmar. The two who had attacked her with Thomas.

Her feet froze on the spot as she stared at the two. That made three people who had to be here to get her. Darie hadn't mentioned the other two, only Thomas. He must have told them he'd found her and she'd sicced the lawmen after him. Her feet wouldn't move when her anger wanted to walk out there and slap the two of them. They had ruined her life once. She wasn't going to let them do it again.

She finally moved, pushing Beau down the bar to where Manfred stood.

"What the hel—" Beau growled when she'd stopped pushing.

"You look scared," Manfred said, immediately

turning to the room and scanning.

"The two that…you know, with Thomas, are in the saloon," she whispered.

"Where?" The word came out low and harsh as Beau also scanned the room.

"The two dandies sitting at the card table. One has red hair and the other dark." She shuddered. Two more people she had never wanted to see again.

"Manfred, they are not welcome here." Beau moved past her and down the length of the bar to the opening. Manfred met him in the middle of the saloon. They strode over to the card table and each one plucked a man from his seat.

"What's going on?" Delmar asked, swinging his legs as Manfred held him off the ground.

"You are no longer allowed in the Silver Dollar." Beau grabbed Billy by his collar and seat of his pants and shoved him to the door.

"You can't do this. I was winning!" Delmar shouted.

"It's my place, I can do what I want. Both of you keep your faces out of my saloon." Beau tossed the man out the door, and Manfred threw the other one out behind him.

Beau shut the door and turned to the interested crowd. "Go back to what you're doing. If any of you see those two lurking around outside, let me know."

Glasses were raised in solidarity, and Jules started a rollicking tune.

Liesa and Belle returned from upstairs followed by Mrs. Dearling. The three studied Lottie Mae.

Her life was becoming a continuous wave of happiness and fear. There were now three men in town who would do her harm. She was sure of it. She started to shake.

Manfred reached across the bar, rubbing a hand up and down her arm. "You are safe, *schatzi*. I won't let anyone hurt you."

She shook her head. As long as she remained here, the men knew where to find her.

"Manfred, would you walk Mrs. Dearling across the alley to the boarding house? And have her lock the doors once she gets in," Beau said, walking up beside Lottie Mae.

She nodded to Manfred. "Go. Those men may take out their anger on Mrs. Dearling. I'm safe in here." But she couldn't stay in the saloon forever with Beau and Manfred standing watch over her.

Reluctantly, Manfred walked to the backroom blanket where Mrs. Dearling stood. Lottie Mae would have loved to walk through that room with the two and closed herself up in the boarding house. The faces of the men in the room became fuzzy and her head light.

Manfred escorted Mrs. Dearling to the boarding house and told her what had happened. She tsked and promised to lock the doors. He hurried back to the saloon. He hadn't liked the fear in Lottie Mae's eyes.

Pushing through the blanket from the backroom to the saloon, he spotted Beau holding a limp Lottie Mae in his arms. The music had stopped and the room was quiet.

"What happened!" Manfred charged behind the bar, taking Lottie Mae into his arms.

"She collapsed. Take her upstairs to my room. Savannah will know what to do," Beau said.

Manfred took the stairs two at a time and rapped on the door Beau had indicated.

Savannah opened the door and gasped. "My word, what happened?" She led him to the bed.

He settled Lottie Mae on the bed and knelt, holding her hand. "I was escorting Mrs. Dearling to the house and came back to find her like this in Beau's arms."

"Darie, see if there are any smelling salts in the washroom." Savannah eased another pillow under Lottie Mae's limp head and neck. "Something had to bring this on." The reverend's wife stared into his eyes.

"Beau and I tossed two men Lottie said were with the other man who attacked her."

Savannah gasped. "All three men who…are here? In Shady Gulch? No wonder she fainted. She has to be scared out of her wits." Savannah took off Lottie's shoes and pulled a blanket over her to her waist.

"You go tell Beau, he'll have to do without her tonight."

Manfred shook his head. "I'm not leaving her."

She rammed her fisted hands on her hips. Before she could tear into him, a soft knock on the door had her spinning to answer it.

Darie crept up to the bed as Savannah opened the door.

Reverend Webster walked in. "I came to check on you, and Beau told me what happened."

The room was getting too crowded. Manfred held onto Lottie's hand and said, "You two go on home. Darie can stay with me and Lottie."

The reverend crossed the floor, stopping beside him. "Savannah will stay. I'll get a description of the men from Beau and round up Sheriff Blake. There has to be an end to this."

Manfred nodded.

Reverend Webster kissed his wife on the cheek and left the room.

Lottie Mae's hand was warmer than the rest of her. Slowly waking, she realized two large hands held hers. She immediately knew it was Manfred. His were so large, her hand was completely covered. Why was he holding her hand? Why was she lying down? Her eyelids slowly lifted.

Manfred's worried face came into view. She raised her other hand to erase the wrinkles on his forehead.

"*Mien Schatzi*." He leaned down, kissing her cheek.

"I said she'd come around." Savannah stepped into view.

"What happened?" Lottie Mae asked, as Manfred helped her sit up.

"I walked Mrs. Dearling to the house and you were slumped in Beau's arms when I came back." The concern in his eyes set her heart pattering.

Flashes of the evening came back to her. Delmar and Billy had been in the saloon. Beau and Manfred had thrown them out. She'd worked herself into a state…She peered into Manfred's eyes. She couldn't leave. He'd lost a wife and child, she didn't want him to suffer losing her. She wound her arms around his neck and clung to him.

Somehow, they would get through this.

Together.

Chapter Twenty

Beau appeared at the door of his room after the downstairs had quieted. Lottie Mae had insisted she go back to work and both Manfred and Savannah had insisted she didn't. The four, she, Manfred, Savannah, and Darie, talked about the wedding and anything other than the fact Lottie Mae had seen the two men who'd attacked her five years ago.

"Everything is closed up. Come on, Jules, Manfred, and I are escorting all of you to the boarding house." He glanced at Savannah. "Your husband is waiting for you downstairs."

Lottie Mae stood. She had her shoes back on, thanks to Manfred, who hadn't allowed her to do anything herself, except use the commode in the wash room.

Downstairs the other ladies sat in chairs waiting with Jules and Lark.

"I wish my past hadn't shown up to ruin all of your lives," Lottie Mae said.

Manfred put an arm around her shoulders. "This isn't your fault. It has never been your fault."

The ladies all murmured agreement.

While it was nice to know no one blamed her, she couldn't stop the guilt of putting everyone in danger.

Jules stepped into the backroom first, followed by the ladies, Manfred and Lottie Mae, Lark and Savannah, and Beau bringing up the rear.

Out in the alley, Savannah said good-night to everyone and told Darie she'd see her tomorrow as each woman used the privy while the four men watched the alley. That Darie and Savannah would be sewing again tomorrow, meant they would all be kept in the saloon all day again. Her past had put them all in a prison.

Jules knocked on the back door when everyone had used the privy. The lock clicked, and Mrs. Dearling appeared dressed in her robe. Everyone filed into the house. Freedom and Belle stayed in the kitchen. Liesa and Darie excused themselves, climbing the stairs. That left Lottie Mae, the men, and Mrs. Dearling standing in the parlor.

"I'm going to sleep in the parlor tonight," Beau said.

Mrs. Dearling started to narrow her eyes.

"Two more men from Lottie Mae's past came into the saloon. I'm sure by now they know everything about the women who work in the saloon. I don't want them trying to get in here." Beau stopped any argument from the older woman.

"I hate that all of you have to change your lives for

me." Lottie Mae couldn't keep quiet any longer. "I can get on the train tomorrow and go somewhere—"

"Leaving won't keep you safe. They found you once, they will find you again," Beau interrupted.

"Here you have people who care for you. We will keep you safe," Manfred said, pulling her into his arms.

"You can't go on herding us around and keeping us locked up. The other women will come to despise me." Her heart ached thinking the women who had become like sisters to her, could turn on her, just like her real family had. "And there could be other women in this town who are in danger. From what Thomas did to Darie, he is still attacking women."

"Lark and Ty are coming here tomorrow morning to have you and Darie tell him what Thomas did to you. He can be hung for what he did," Beau said.

She curled into Manfred's strong warm body. Thomas had put her through a fate worse than death and now had turned her life upside down, but she wasn't sure she could say the words that would have him killed.

"I will be here, if you wish," Manfred said softly into her ear.

She pushed out of his arms. "No. I don't want you to hear…" She turned pleading eyes on Beau. "Can Savannah be here, instead of Lark? It will be hard enough to tell Ty. He has always… well, his presence makes me nervous." She knew Darie hadn't met the sheriff yet and hoped he would leave his hubris outside the door.

"I know he's pushy when it comes to women." Beau studied her and then Manfred. "Would it make it easier if I talk him into letting you tell Lark and

Savannah? Savannah can write down what you say."

She nodded her head. Lark was a preacher and had never made her feel uncomfortable like the sheriff had. "I'm sure it would help Darie."

"I'll speak to Ty first thing in the morning." Beau stepped toward the door. "Manfred, Jules, figure out who is watching the house first."

Even though she'd spent all evening with Manfred, she wasn't ready for him to leave. "Can Manfred do the first watch?" She peered up into the blacksmith's face. "I'll be able to fall asleep easier knowing he's outside."

Beau opened the door. "You heard the lady. She wants Manfred on first watch."

Jules walked out the door, but Lottie Mae clung to Manfred's hand.

"*Schatzi*, I cannot stay in the house as much as I would like to be with you." Manfred put a hand under her chin and kissed her lips lightly. "Look out your window before you go to bed and you will see me." He extracted his hand from hers and stepped out.

Beau closed the door.

Her heart sunk.

Manfred watched the windows on the second floor of the boarding house. Ten minutes after leaving Lottie, he spotted a light go on, one window over from what he thought was her room. Her silhouette in the window could be seen before the curtains moved slightly and she peered down at him. He waved and smiled.

She waved back, and the curtain dropped into place.

He found a barrel in the alley and placed it where he could lean against the privy with his back while sitting on the barrel. He could see the back door of the boarding house and Lottie's window.

The way the two men he and Beau had thrown out of the saloon were dressed, they had to be staying in one of the hotels. But if they were, why hadn't the reverend and sheriff found them? After Lottie and Darie gave their accounts of their attacks, the three men would be behind bars. No longer a threat to anyone.

He caught sight of something moving at the other corner of the house. Would the men be *verrückt*, crazy, enough to try and get to Lottie? He didn't want to leave the back door unwatched, but he also wanted to see who was walking around the house.

Manfred walked quietly down the alley to the other corner of the house and looked. There was a man walking along the side in the shadow. He wore a hat with a wide brim like the sheriff and the cattlemen wore. He tried to remember if he'd seen any of the men they were watching wear that type of hat. The two in the saloon tonight had worn hats with the narrow brim of a businessman.

He glanced to the back door. It was locked but that wouldn't stop someone set on trouble. One last glance at the area behind the boarding house, he strode down the side of the house, stopping before he stepped out in the open. Manfred peered around the corner and recognized the person standing in front of the house. It was one of the deputies.

Pivoting, he strode along the house to the back. He took his place back on the barrel and continued watching Lottie's window and the back door.

He'd started to nod off when Jules stepped out of the back of the saloon and relieved him.

He was glad Lottie had insisted he take the first watch but now he had to get sleep. He planned to be nearby in the morning in case she needed him.

Lottie Mae woke and stretched. She'd fallen asleep counting all the ways Manfred made her happy. Movement in the hall reminded her Beau planned to have her and Darie talk about their attacks. Her belly tightened, and her hands shook. She hoped he was able to talk the sheriff into letting Savannah and Lark listen. She wouldn't be able to say a thing with the sheriff in the room.

Her door opened and Darie entered, her eyes wide. "Beau says we have to tell the reverend and his wife what happened to us."

Lottie Mae patted her bed. Darie crossed the room and crawled onto the bed, curling under Lottie Mae's arm. She embraced the younger, smaller woman.

"We can't go on living with fear. We have to tell them what happened so the law can deal with the men who hurt us.

"I don't think I can talk about it." Darie's body shook. Her attack had been more recent.

"I'll go first. Maybe that will give you the strength to tell your story when you see Lark and Savannah won't treat me or you any differently. These men are our enemies, not the reverend and his wife."

Darie shifted and peered into her eyes. "If you tell them your story, I won't have to say anything."

She shook her head. "We both need to speak up about Thomas. Otherwise, he could say I am lying. That he doesn't remember five years ago. But if you also accuse him, he won't be able to talk his way out of it."

The younger woman didn't act convinced.

"If we don't do this, we will be scared the rest of our lives. Do you want to live that way? You've been cooped up in here or the saloon ever since you arrived. There are people your age you could be visiting with and activities you could be attending if you didn't have to hide."

Lottie Mae urged the younger woman to the edge of the bed. "I'm getting up, getting dressed, and eating breakfast. I want to be ready when Lark and Savannah arrive." She was acting braver than she felt, but if she didn't, Darie wouldn't speak up and she'd be the only one accusing Thomas.

Lark and Savannah sat on the settee in the parlor. Lottie Mae and Darie were in the chairs, facing them. Savannah had a school tablet on her lap and a pencil in her hand.

Beau had escorted them into the parlor and closed the door.

Lark cleared his throat. "I know this isn't going to be easy and if it will help I can stand in a corner out of your sight."

Unsure what her feelings were or how she would react to his presence, she nodded. It might be easier thinking she was only talking to Savannah and Darie.

The reverend stood and moved out of her sight. She knew he was still in the room from the squeak of him sitting in the rocking chair.

Her hands twisted together as she gathered the courage to begin.

Savannah patted her knee.

One by one the words crawled up her throat and

slipped past her lips. She told of the scolding she'd given the three boys, Thomas's threat, and her walk home from sending the telegraph.

Darie squeaked as she told of having her skirts wrapped around her head. The feeling of no air and the pain. Tears trickled down her cheeks as she remembered lying on the ground, her lower body exposed, and not breathing—hoping the silence meant they had gone. She'd lain there for nearly ten minutes before shoving her dress down, pulling her drawers up, and hobbling home in a torn and dirty dress.

Darie patted her arm.

Lottie Mae swiped at the tears with the backs of her hands and stared at the paper full of words. "I'll sign that."

Savannah turned the tablet to her, and she signed her name. After revisiting that day, she hoped they'd all three hang.

"Would you like some tea before Darie gives her account?" Savannah asked. Her voice sounding strangled.

Lottie Mae shook her head. She didn't want Darie to lose her courage if they stopped to have tea. She reached over, taking the younger woman's hand. "You can do it. Telling someone makes it feel less of a burden on yourself," Lottie Mae said, hoping to show Darie it had helped her.

When Darie acted as if she didn't know where to start, Lottie Mae asked, "Where did you first meet him?"

"On the train. He was already sitting down when I boarded. He offered a seat next to him, but I took a seat with an older woman and her husband. At one of the stops, I left the train to walk. My legs were cramped from sitting so much. He came upon me then, offering a sweet and conversation. He seemed well-educated and talked of seeing places I'd only read about." She stared down at her hands. "When he invited me to walk to the back of the train and he'd show me the constellations, I thought that was what he wanted to do. I'd thought to that point he was an honorable man." She hiccupped, and her fingers twisted together. "When he stopped in the baggage car, I thought he was going to get a looking glass to better see the stars." She gulped, stared at Lottie Mae, and opened her mouth. No noise emitted.

"What happened in the baggage car?" Lottie Mae asked, hoping Darie could tell enough to prove they weren't making up the stories.

"He-he told me to look for something down low, and he tossed my skirt over my head, holding me bent and…that's when…" Darie stared at Savannah.

"What did he do?" Savannah asked softly, her face paler than Lottie Mae had ever seen it.

"It hurt. I've never had such pain. I screamed but it was muffled in my skirt and he slapped my backside and told me to be quiet. The pain came again, and I couldn't stop the scream. He gripped my sides so hard, I could barely breathe. He said he'd kill me if I told anyone and then shoved in me until I thought sure I would split in two. I think I passed out from the pain. The next thing I remember was rolling across the ground and the train's sounds growing fainter."

Savannah had tears trickling down her cheeks as she turned the tablet to Darie to sign.

The rocking chair creaked. Lark came back into

view. "Lottie Mae, what are the names of the three men?"

"Thomas Decker is who assaulted me and Darie. Delmar Jones and Billy Norbett are the other two who assaulted me."

"Savannah write the names across the top of the page and their victims."

Savannah did as her husband told her. Then they both signed as witnesses to the statements.

Lark held out his hand to Lottie Mae. She placed her hand in his. "I've known your past but not the full measure of the hurt. God helped Beau find you. I know you will find a better life and new wonderful memories with Manfred."

He turned to Darie. He reached for her hand, but she held it back. "I wish I could say the Lord had a reason for what happened to you, but I can't think of any good that came of what that man did to you. I'll pray for you to find your way back from this ordeal."

She stared at him.

Savannah handed the tablet to her husband and pulled Darie and Lottie Mae into a hug. "Neither of you should have gone through that. You are strong women to be able to tell your story and get rid of such a vile man."

The minute the door opened and Lark stepped out, Manfred appeared. He strode straight for Lottie Mae, embracing her.

She wrapped her arms around him, enjoying his solidness and strength.

"Are you all right?" he asked.

"I am now." She snuggled closer and wished she

didn't have to work at the saloon or try and avoid the three men.

The sound of people leaving the room made her heart sing. Perhaps, she and Manfred would get some time alone. She peeked out from where she was snuggled and found them blissfully alone.

"If we closed the door, how long do you think it would take Mrs. Dearling to barge in?" Manfred asked.

She giggled. She'd been thinking the same thing. "We could give it a try."

He placed her on the settee and crossed the room, quietly closing the door. Manfred returned to a spot beside her. He pulled her into his arms and kissed her.

This was what she wanted every day. To be loved and cherished by this man. But that wasn't going to happen until her past was put away for good.

She wrapped her arms around his neck, pressing as close as she could get. He was her salvation and her future.

His hands on her back pressed her closer. One hand slid up to the back of her head, tipping her head slightly, his tongue parting her lips, and…heaven help her, she followed his actions, sliding her tongue against his, tasting coffee and Manfred.

She moaned, and he drew out of the kiss.

"Shhh…We must be quiet to continue this way." His head tipped back to hers when the sound of Mrs. Dearling's heels clacked down the hall toward the parlor.

She shoved against his chest, sitting upright and settling her skirt around her legs. Manfred shifted and crossed one leg. One arm remained across the top of the settee behind her.

The door opened. Mrs. Dearling poked her head in. Her gaze hopped back and forth between them several times before she said, "You should keep the door open if you don't want people talking." She disappeared, leaving the door open.

Manfred dropped his arm over her shoulders, drawing her to him. He kissed the tip of her nose and peered into her eyes. "Lottie, I am getting anxious to have you all to myself."

She kissed his chin. "As am I."

His eyes lit up. "Would you like to pick a day to wed?"

Nothing would have made her happier than to tell the world they were to be married soon. However, she didn't feel right marrying Manfred until her past was settled. "I would like nothing more, but we must wait. I want to make sure there is no one to spoil our future."

"I would rather marry you and have you by my side night and day." Manfred grasped her hand. "I will follow your wishes but as soon as you are ready, I will be at the church waiting for you."

She laughed. "And I'll be running to the church."

Chapter Twenty-one

Everyone was escorted to the Silver Dollar when it opened. Darie and Savannah went up to Beau's room to work on Lottie Mae's wedding dress.

Lottie Mae took her now usual place behind the bar. She wasn't sure if she was allowed the privilege of hiding behind the bar because Manfred wished to marry her or to keep her safe in case the men from her past snuck in.

Lark entered the saloon. He walked over to where she stood at the bar. "You might want to go change. I'm here to escort you over to the school. The superintendent arrived on the train and would like to interview you."

Her heart stopped, and her hands shook. When she'd let Beau talk her into interviewing for the teaching position, she never dreamed she'd have to go before the superintendent.

"I can't go today. I don't know…"

"If you don't come today, you won't get the job." Lark shook his head as Beau walked up beside them.

"Why did Lottie Mae turn white?" Beau asked.

"The superintendent is here to interview potential teachers." Lark nodded toward Lottie Mae. "She isn't ready."

"Yes, she is." Beau grabbed her shoulders, making her face him. "You need to put the past behind you. This is a step toward getting out of this saloon. You have to take it."

She swallowed. She wanted out, had for nearly a year, but didn't know how. This was her chance. Could be her only chance, if she wanted to marry Manfred and remain in this town with her friends. She straightened her shoulders and nodded. "I'll go change."

Lark followed her out the back of the saloon. Outside, sunlight glinted off the handgun in a holster slung low on his hip. He was the only gun packing reverend she'd ever met. But then he was also the only outlaw turned preacher she'd ever met.

He waited in the parlor while she went up to change.

Lottie Mae donned her best skirt and blouse. She recombed her hair and put it back up in a bun. With one last look in the mirror, she picked up her reticule and hurried down the stairs.

A wide body blocked her way as she hurried into the parlor.

She grinned.

Manfred pivoted, a responding smile on his face. "I heard the superintendent came in on the train. I went to the saloon. Beau told me the good news."

His mention of why she was hurrying tamped down her good humor. "I hope I make a good impression on him."

"*Schatzi*, you will." Manfred grasped her gloved hand and kissed her knuckles. "Do you wish that I walk with you?"

She glanced at Lark and knew they wouldn't be able to shake him. He, no doubt, had orders from his wife and brother-in-law to not leave her side.

"I would like to be escorted by two such respected men." She slipped her arm through Manfred's, and Lark stepped past them to the front door.

Walking down the street to the school, she could imagine what it would feel like to be treated like the other respectable women in town. While she hadn't been reviled like the women in the other saloons, she still had been on the sour end of looks and leers.

At the school, Manfred grasped her hand. "Good luck."

"Thank you."

He released her hand, and she walked up to the school house door. Lark opened the door for her and entered behind.

She blinked a minute, getting eyes that had been bathed in sunlight to adjust to the dim entrance and cloak room. Lark touched her elbow, leading her into the school room.

The desks all in a row and the smell of chalk dust started her heart fluttering. She'd loved teaching. Seeing the faces of her students light up when they grasped reading or cyphering. This felt like coming home.

As her gaze swept the room, she caught her first glimpse of the man bent over inspecting a book on the teacher's desk. The sight nearly had her spinning and running for the door. At her initial glance, the man had reminded her of the superintendent who had believed the young men over her five short years ago.

He raised up, standing a good head taller than her past accuser. He also had kind eyes and a ready smile. His bald head with a band of hair just above his ears had been the only likeness to the other superintendent.

He stepped around the desk with an outstretched hand. "I'm Mr. Pendergast, the superintendent of this district."

She shook hands. "Lottie Mae Peck."

"Reverend, good to see you again." Mr. Pendergast shook hands with Lark. "Are you here to vouch for this woman?" The smile on the man's face said he was joking.

"I'm sure once you visit with her and see her qualifications, you won't need a recommendation from me." Lark walked back down the aisle of desks and disappeared through the cloak room door.

"Have a seat," the man offered.

Lottie Mae sat in the desk and chair at the front of the room. Her hands sweat so much her grip on the front of the desk kept slipping.

"Miss Peck…It is Miss?" Mr. Pendergast asked.

"Currently, but I'll be marrying Mr. Albrecht soon." Her cheeks heated at the mention of Manfred.

"Does that mean the two of you will continue to live in Shady Gulch?" He picked up the paper she'd brought to the school the day Beau had goaded her into applying for the position.

"Yes. Man…Mr. Albrecht is the blacksmith in town. We both like it here and don't plan to move."

"Good. I really don't like having to hire a new teacher every year. It's hard on the students and hard on the community." He grinned. "Not to mention it takes me away from home."

"I understand." She smiled. The man's warm smile and eyes made her feel comfortable.

"It says here you haven't taught for five years. Why is that?"

Her throat tightened.

"You have a certificate from a reputable teaching school," he said, as if noting her unease with his previous question.

"There was an altercation five years ago. The superintendent wasn't willing to hear both sides of the problem and I was dismissed." She swallowed. "I have been teaching adults while in Shady Gulch and miss teaching the children." This was all true without telling him about being shamed.

"I see. Some superintendents take their job too seriously." He winked. "What curriculum have you used in the past?"

The rest of the interview went well. By the time she walked out of the building, she had a feeling she had the job. Mr. Pendergast had been impressed with her ciphering and penmanship.

Manfred and Lark stood outside the door, visiting. They both turned at the same time.

"You have the position?" Manfred asked.

"I won't know until he visits with the other woman who is also seeking the position. But he seemed pleased with my answers." She wanted to twirl and shout but didn't know if the man was watching.

"We will celebrate with a nice dinner at the Allman Hotel," Manfred said, placing her hand on his arm.

"I wish you could," Lark said, stepping up to them. "That's the hotel where two of the men we're protecting Lottie Mae from have been staying. Mr. Allman swore they are no longer there, but we can't take chances."

Her euphoria dampened as if Lark had dumped a bucket of cold water on her head. "Why hasn't Sheriff Blake locked them up?"

"They disappeared after Beau and Manfred threw them out of the saloon."

"No one has seen them?" She wanted to be happy she had a job, not fearing for her safety.

"They may have left town but we have to be careful. I'm sure Savannah can make a celebratory dinner," Lark said, motioning for them to walk to the street.

She shook her head. "I don't want to put Savannah or anyone else out." She gazed up at Manfred. "I'd like to have a picnic on your property."

He grinned. "You make the food, I'll get the buggy and come by for you."

That he was so willing to stop his work and join her, started her heart thumping against her ribs. "I can do that."

Lark held out his arm. "Then I'll escort you back to the boarding house."

"We have one stop to make on the way. I have to tell Beau I won't be back to the saloon tonight."

Manfred whistled as he strode down the street to his blacksmith shop. He would close up for the day, clean up, and rent a buggy from Mr. Montgomery. The idea of spending time alone with Lottie was enough to make his body heat and his desires emerge like a roaring bear that had been in hibernation. He knew he couldn't hold or touch her as he craved. Not yet. Not until he could prove he wouldn't hurt her.

But the thought of holding her in his arms caused intense pleasure. He closed the big doors on his building and wandered into his small bedroom. He washed with a cloth and the wash basin and put on his Sunday shirt and trousers. He had few clothes because he had to have them special made by a seamstress. Nothing ready-made fit his long legs or broad shoulders. Did Lottie sew? It didn't matter.

Once he was cleaned up, he walked over to the livery and found Mr. Montgomery. "I would like to rent the same buggy and horse as the other day."

"That's twice in one week and you ain't never rented a buggy from me before. You gettin' sweet on someone?" The man had never been one of Manfred's friends and his talk now wasn't going to make it happen.

"My reasons are not of importance to you." Manfred walked out to the corral and found the horse from the other day. It had handled well. If he built a house at the spring, Lottie would need a way to get to town. He would ask if the horse and buggy were for sale when the time came.

Mr. Montgomery brought the harness over to the buggy. Together they had the animal harnessed to the buggy in short time.

Manfred handed the man a silver dollar. "Thank you. I will have them back to you before dark."

He climbed into the buggy and headed the horse down the main street of town. No sense in letting the man see him go straight to the boarding house.

Passing the Silver Dollar Saloon, Beau stood in the doorway. He waved and smiled. The saloon proprietor must not be upset with him taking away one of his ladies.

At the corner, he turned the buggy and headed for the front of the boarding house.

Lottie stood on the porch, a basket covered with a blanket at her feet.

He leaped off the buggy and strode up to the porch. "Your face glows like the spring sun."

Her cheeks deepened in color. "It is because I see a future that doesn't include the Silver Dollar."

Manfred nodded and picked up the basket. He offered his arm to Lottie. She slipped her hand through the crook of his elbow and they walked back to the buggy. He placed the basket and blanket in the space behind the seat and helped Lottie Mae onto the seat.

With her by his side, he continued up the street, past his shop, and over the railroad tracks. This would be the best afternoon and evening, he'd had since leaving Chicago.

"Was Beau upset you were not helping tonight?" he asked.

"At first. But he also knows how much I've wanted to go back to teaching and how much spending time with you means to me." Her cheeks blushed prettily, and her lashes lowered, hiding her emotions from him.

He grinned. It had been a long time since he'd considered how pretty a woman looked. Or how one reacted to him. He reached over, picking up her hand. "That you wish to spend time with me, makes me very happy."

She glanced at his hand holding hers and into his eyes.

The desire he witnessed in her gaze made him swallow and steady his beating heart.

To take his mind off where it had leapt to, he asked, "What questions did the superintendent ask?"

He listened to her account of her interview not really hearing the words but hanging on the lilt of her tone. She was happy with the outcome, he'd known that from her reactions when she'd exited the school. But to hear the happiness in her voice, he would do whatever it took to keep that there.

"He did ask why I hadn't taught for five years." She turned, her knees touching his thigh, her gaze intent on his. "I said the superintendent hadn't been openminded enough to hear both sides." She clutched his hand with both of hers. "Do you think that was the right thing to say?"

Manfred pulled the buggy to a stop. He disengaged his hand from hers and cradled her head in his hands. "How did you feel about his answer?" He didn't want her doubting herself.

"He chuckled and said some superintendents were full of themselves." She relaxed.

"Then he understands some people are not good listeners." He leaned down, kissed her softly on the lips, and retreated before his body overruled his mind.

Picking up the reins, he started the buggy back in

motion.

Lottie slid her knees to face forward. He glanced out of the corner of his eye. She wore a smile.

Chapter Twenty-two

The sun started its descent in the sky as Lottie Mae leaned against Manfred. His arms held her close as they reclined against a boulder, listening to the trickle of the spring and the sounds of the birds settling in for the night.

"This is so peaceful," she said, in a whisper. She didn't want to speak any louder and ruin the intimacy of the moment.

"It is perfect," he whispered in her ear. His warm breath heated the tender skin behind her ear.

She shivered.

"Are you cold?" he drew her up onto his lap, her legs resting on his.

"No." She rolled in his arms, causing her breasts to press against his hard chest and her back to arch, pressing the juncture of her legs against his manhood. She froze at the realization he was hard and the pressure caused throbbing in her body.

"*Schatzi*, you stir my body to life. But now is not the time to show you how much." He gently turned her sideways, holding her on his lap like a child. He grasped her chin and pressed his lips to hers.

Any other man, she would have shot off his lap or fought. But she knew Manfred cared enough about her to tamp out his urges and show her what she yearned for but feared.

His tongue slid across the seam of her lips and she opened. A moan escaped as he slipped in, caressing her tongue as the hand holding her chin, slipped to the back of her head angling her mouth to deepen the kiss. His other hand had captured a breast. She pressed into his hand as something brushed back and forth over her sensitive nipple under her blouse and chemise.

Her body caught fire. She moaned and thrust her tongue into Manfred's mouth. He tasted of the roast beef sandwich and sweet intoxication. She moaned again, her hands squeezing and molding the hard muscles of Manfred's back and chest. She wanted to feel his skin. Her hand slipped into the neck of his shirt and encountered slick skin and a sprinkle of hair.

He pulled out of the kiss, drawing her hand out of his clothing. "*Schatzi*, we should return. If this goes on, I will not be able to control myself. I do not wish you to think I am an animal."

Bereavement is what she experienced when he put space between them. She never wanted to be parted from him.

"I wish to continue." She pressed her body toward him.

Manfred shook his head and stared in her eyes. "To continue would mean I would lay you down and love you here, in this beautiful place. This I wish to do, but not now, not your first time with me. I am big and heavy. I do not wish to hurt you."

Her fevered body, still throbbed and yearned, but her mind snapped to his words. "Make love? Hurt?"

When she started to pull away, he held her and peered into her eyes. "It is what a man and woman do when they love one another."

"Hurt each other?"

He shook his head, his face somber. "No. To love and share our bodies is to soar and feel complete. But I fear my size will hurt you."

"Making love doesn't hurt?" Ever since her assault she'd equated the coming together of a man and woman to pain and fear.

His face softened, and his eyes sparkled. "*Mien schatzi*, to come together with a person you love is freeing and life changing."

"You had that with your wife?" She wasn't sure if she envied his first wife for having had the experience with Manfred first or sorrow that she died because she loved him so much.

"Yes. My Nina and I soared in the clouds." His smile turned sad. "I would have given up that feeling if it would have kept her alive."

Lottie Mae studied the man. He had loved his wife deeply. Would he ever feel the same for her? Would he help her break through her fears of intimacy or would he abstain to keep her alive? But then would that mean he loved her more than Nina or less?

She scrambled out of his arms and stood. "We

should go." There was much she had to think about. The way his kisses and touch brought her body to life and whether or not he loved her with the same intensity that she loved him.

Manfred wasn't sure how to react to Lottie's sudden quietness. She'd allowed him to help fold the blanket and escort her to the buggy, but her silence had him wondering what he'd said or done.

"Are you mad at me?" he finally asked.

She glanced at him. "No. I'm not mad. I'm thinking."

"What about?" He had to know if he'd overstepped somewhere. He had wanted to lay her down and love her with every drop of his blood, but his mind had held him back. She'd proven she had a fiery side to her that would match his enthusiasm in bed, but he didn't want to hurt her. Should she prove as fragile as Nina, he'd have to restrain his need for her.

"Us."

He glanced at her, watched her cheeks slowly darken. "What about us?"

"I-it's not something we should discuss." The discomfort in her voice put a smile on his face and urged his mischievous side to rise.

"What can we not discuss? We are betrothed are we not?" He raised one eyebrow.

She twisted, once again, pressing her knees against his thighs and sending his body into a spin.

"I wonder at the size of you," her gaze flitted to his crotch and his growing *schwanz,* "that you fear hurting me."

Her words and actions proved to him that she was

willing to be loved by him. This lightened his heart. "There are many ways you could be hurt. Ja, I am bigger than most men, not just here," he pointed to his crotch, "but all over. I do not wish to get so caught up in the feelings that I crush you with my weight or squeeze you too hard with my arms."

She grasped his arm. "You would never do that. You are gentle and kind."

"You are truly *mien schatzi*, my treasure." He kissed her lips and urged the horse into a trot. She should be home and away from his growing desires for her. Their wedding night would be soon enough to show her how much he wanted her.

Lottie Mae walked up the steps of the boarding house on Manfred's arm. It had been the perfect ending to the day. "Thank you for the picnic. It was wonderful." She turned to him as he placed the basket and blanket on the chair.

"You deserve a wonderful day every day." He took her hands. "I cannot wait until the day you become my wife. We will not have to part as the day ends."

Her heart warmed at his words. "That day can't come too soon for me."

He smiled and leaned down, placing a chaste kiss on her lips. "I will see you tomorrow."

She watched him walk down to the buggy, climb in, and wave before heading down the street.

The sun finished disappearing beyond the horizon and she sighed. Nothing could spoil this day.

She opened the screen, holding it with her body and put her hand on the door knob to the house when a creak behind her tightened all her muscles.

"You play hookey from the saloon to give your body to that man?" Thomas asked from behind her.

"I have never given my body to a man. It has only been taken." She turned and pushed on the door to rush in, but a hand grasped her arm, jerking her away from the door.

"You told too many people lies about me. You're goin' to pay for that." He jerked her body against him.

She screamed and stomped on his foot.

"You bitch!" His hand made a grab for her face, but she ducked and screamed again.

The door flew open. Mrs. Dearling stood in the opening with a rifle. "Get your hands off Lottie Mae!"

The man threw his arms in the air, and Lottie Mae darted around behind Mrs. Dearling. She ran down the hall, out the back door, and down the alley. She didn't stop running until she came to the blacksmith shop.

She flung the door open and stumbled through the shop and into the back room where Manfred slept. He hadn't made it home from taking the horse and buggy back. But that was fine. She wasn't sure she wanted a man right now, but she knew Manfred would keep her safe.

Chapter Twenty-three

Manfred spotted the door standing open as he approached his shop. After the attempted fire, he walked around the building before slipping in the door. His eyes had become accustomed to the darkness while searching the outside. He didn't see anyone lurking in the corners. However, he took his time moving into the room where he slept.

Cautiously, he grasped the leather tong that raised the iron bar on the inside of the door. When the bar had cleared the cradle, he inched the door open. Someone sat on his bed. From the silhouette, he deemed it to be a woman.

"Who is here?" he asked at the same moment his nostrils registered the scent of Lottie.

"Manfred!" She lunged at him, her arms wrapping around his waist.

He held her trembling body, relishing the way she

clung to him but worried at the reason why she had run to his place after he'd just left her.

"*Schatzi*, what is wrong?" he asked, grasping her head and tipping it up, to look at her in the moonlight barely sifting through the window. His fingers encountered wet trails of tears on her cheeks. "Why do you weep? And why did you seek me out?"

"He was there." Her body trembled.

He gathered her into his arms and settled on the bed, holding her on his lap like a frightened child. "Who was where?"

"Thomas…"

The name bunched his muscles. "Where?"

"He came up behind me as I was opening the door to the boarding house." Her body tensed.

"Did he hurt you? I did not see anyone as I drove away." He chastised himself for not seeing her inside the door. He'd been so overwhelmed by the feelings she evoked in his body, he'd only thought of putting space between them before he brought shame to them both.

"He grabbed me. Said I told too many people about him." She trembled.

"How did you get away?" He couldn't believe the animosity the man held for Lottie to attack her in front of the boarding house.

"Mrs. Dearling heard me scream and came to the door with a rifle." She pushed away from him. "I left her dealing with that man. And Darie!" She fisted her hands. "I was so scared I ran here looking for you. What if I left them at that man's mercy?"

"Come on. We will go see if the man did them harm." Manfred tucked her against his side. He closed both doors behind them, and they hurried down the street toward the boarding house. A hundred feet away, they could see all the lights in the house were ablaze.

Lottie Mae started to push away from him.

"No, you stay beside me until we know all is safe." He held her close as they entered through the front door.

Voices came from the kitchen. He moved cautiously until he recognized Beau's booming voice and that of Sheriff Blake.

Stepping through the doorway, all gazes landed on them. Mrs. Dearling, Darie, Doctor Nolan, Sheriff Blake, and Beau.

"Where the hell have you been?" Beau asked, taking a step toward her.

Manfred slipped Lottie Mae behind him. "She ran to my shop when the man tried to take her." He stood nearly chest to chest with the saloon owner. He knew Beau cared for the women who worked at the saloon, but he wouldn't allow even Beau to hurt or upset Lottie.

Sheriff Blake put a hand on Beau's shoulder, pulling him back. "I need Lottie Mae to tell me what happened. My deputy is out looking for the man."

Lottie tapped his back, and he stepped aside. She didn't shake anymore, and her eyes blazed with anger. "Manfred dropped me off after our picnic. It was just about dark. I watched him drive away—"

"You didn't make sure she was in the house!" Beau bellowed, taking a step toward Manfred.

Manfred dropped his chin to his chest. "We spoke of so many good things, I forgot about the man. It is my fault."

"No, it isn't! I knew better than to stand on the

porch watching you drive away and then watching the sunset." Lottie Mae grabbed a fistful of his shirt sleeve. Making him look at her. "This wasn't your fault."

He wanted to believe her, but he knew he should have made sure she was in the house and the door locked.

"What happened?" Sheriff Blake asked, ignoring all of them but Lottie Mae.

"I opened the screen door and put my hand on the door knob when Thomas grabbed me from behind and said…" She swallowed twice and glanced at everyone before looking at the ground. "He said I told too many people lies about him and I was going to pay." Fear made her voice squeak.

Manfred reached out, pulling her to his side. He wouldn't allow anyone to hurt her. Not even himself.

Lottie Mae appreciated Manfred's protectiveness, but right now, with all of the eyes on her, she was uncomfortable with how casually he pulled her to his side. She squirmed a bit and stepped forward. "I stomped on his foot. He cursed and threatened me. I screamed. Mrs. Dearling must have heard it—"

"I did, too," Dr. Nolan interrupted.

She nodded to the man. "Mrs. Dearling had a rifle. He released me, and I ran through the house, down the alley, and to the blacksmith shop. I let myself in and waited for Manfred."

Sheriff Blake spun on Manfred. "Where were you?"

"I took the horse and buggy back to the livery." He glared at the sheriff.

"When Dr. Nolan arrived at the porch, the stranger

glared at me, said he'd be seeing me and all the…ladies of the house and ran off." Mrs. Dearling's face paled as she recounted what had happened.

Sheriff Blake faced Beau. "We have to find this man and do something to get rid of him. It sounds like no one in this house is safe until we do."

Beau nodded.

Lottie Mae shivered. No one in this house or anyone she came in contact with would be safe until Thomas Decker was in jail or dead.

"I have to get back to the saloon. Jules is in there alone. If this Decker and his friends walked in there, he'd be at a disadvantage." Beau put a hand on her arm. "Stay in this house until we all go to the saloon tomorrow."

She nodded, but her gaze was on Manfred. There were things she needed to say to him, in private.

Beau left through the back door. The sheriff and doctor walked out the front door.

Lottie Mae grasped Manfred's hand. "We'll be in the parlor," she said to Mrs. Dearling and Darie before she led him down the hall to the room at the front of the house.

"Sit," she told him, motioning to the settee. When he'd sat, she plopped on the cushion beside him. "You can't blame yourself for my lack of judgement. I'd had such a wonderful time, I'd forgotten to be cautious."

"I am to blame. The stranger had slipped my mind as well." He put a large palm against her face. "I could never live with myself had he hurt you."

She smiled. "He won't hurt me. There are too many people who will protect me." She thought of Mrs. Dearling, who only weeks ago, Lottie Mae had felt was getting too old to take care of the house, then the way the older woman had sounded unflappable, holding that rifle on Thomas. If only she had that much bravery when it came to the man.

"I should protect you. I will protect you." Manfred's nostrils flared as he vowed her protection.

He was so strong in both body and mind, it stole her breath. He wished to marry her and would vow to honor and protect her. But she didn't want him getting hurt in the process.

"There is only so much one person can do." She didn't want to send him away, but she knew any minute Mrs. Dearling would walk through the door and suggest it was time for him to leave.

"I will be safe in the house tonight. Go rest." She stood, drawing him to his feet as well.

"I won't rest. I will be outside, watching." He put a hand behind her head, drawing her to her toes as he leaned down and pressed his lips to hers.

What she thought would be a soft kiss, turned into a mind blurring, body throbbing, re-awakening of all the sensations he'd conjured in her before.

"It's time for Manfred to leave," Mrs. Dearling's voice boomed through the swirling in Lottie Mae's head.

Manfred lowered her to the settee. "I will be outside. You will be safe." He disappeared. She heard the front door open and close and still couldn't find the strength in her legs to stand.

Mrs. Dearling sat beside her. "He's a good man. He loves you." The older, wiser woman's face softened. "It's a magical thing when two people fall in love." Her dreamy gaze narrowed. She stared into Lottie Mae's eyes. "But while your head is in the clouds, you still need to be vigilant. That man who tried to take you tonight is nothing but pure evil. You and Manfred need to be careful."

Chapter Twenty-four

Sheriff Blake knocked on the back door and walked in with Manfred on his heels as Mrs. Dearling placed breakfast on the table.

Lottie Mae was happy to see Manfred until she saw how tired he looked. He had stayed out in the alley all night, watching. She hated that Thomas had brought this upon them all.

She immediately took Manfred's arm, placing him at the opposite end of the table from where Beau was seated. She poured him a cup of coffee. When she placed it on the table in front of him, his arm snaked around her waist and he leaned his head on her shoulder.

"Thank you. I will not be much good at my shop today." He picked up the cup and sipped, his arm still around her.

Her cheeks grew warm until she realized no one

was paying any attention to them. Ty and Beau had their heads together at the far end of the table, and the women were all filling their plates as quietly as possible. She smiled. They were trying to listen into the conversation between Beau and the sheriff. All their lives were in danger thanks to the monster who had attacked her and Darie.

"I can't believe you haven't found this man," Beau said loud enough for them all to hear.

Sheriff Blake slapped his hand on the table, making the dishes nearest him jump and rattle. "He's slipperier than a catfish. Pete spent the night looking through the hotels and behind every building."

Beau stood up. "Did he try the Mad Dog? Flanagan would hide his mother's killer for a price."

"I was headed there after breakfast." Sheriff Blake narrowed his eyes as he raised his cup of coffee. "You aren't going with me. You and Cullen always get in a fight."

"Beau, sit down," Mrs. Dearling said, placing her hands on her hips. "I want this over with without anyone in this house getting hurt."

"I will go with you, Sheriff," Manfred said.

Lottie Mae's heart stopped. She wanted to ask him not to go but knew her words would fall on deaf ears. He wanted this over as well. "Be careful," she said as he stood.

He smiled. "The law is on our side. Sheriff, I am ready."

Sheriff Blake nodded and stood. He grabbed his hat from the pegs by the door and the two disappeared.

When she turned her gaze back to the room all eyes were on her. "I'm sorry I brought this trouble to you all.”

Darie shook her head. “It wasn’t you. It was me.”

“No! It wasn’t.” Lottie Mae moved to Darie’s side.

“Neither one of you brought that man here. He came by train and brought his evil with him,” Mrs. Dearling said.

“Ty and Manfred will get to the bottom of this. Until then, you all remain in the house. Either myself, Jules, or Lark will escort you to the saloon at two.” Beau studied Mrs. Dearling and Darie. “That includes both of you.”

Manfred’s eyes felt as if shards of iron had landed in them. They burned, and his eyelids were heavy as the sledge hammer he wielded to make iron bend to his will. But he wouldn’t be able to sleep until they’d taken away the threat to Lottie Mae and all the women in the boarding house.

At the Mad Dog, Sheriff Blake pushed the door open.

The rancid cigar smoke, stale beer, and body odor opened Manfred’s eyes. The stench, darkness, and feeling he’d stepped into a den of sin, chilled his skin. The only saloon he’d ever set foot in was the Silver Dollar. Now he understood why some of the men who entered were struck with awe. Beau’s establishment was like stepping into a church compared to this filthy room.

“What are you doin’ here so early of a mornin’, Sheriff?” asked a tall, thin man with a balding head, big bushy mustache, and dark eyes.

“Cullen, we’re looking for a man who attacked a woman last night. Any chance I can get a look around?”

Sheriff Blake didn't wait for an answer, putting his foot on the bottom step of the stairs.

"This be my property and I don't care for the likes of you comin' here and rilin' up my payin' customers," the man said in an Irish accent as he skipped up two steps above the sheriff.

"Manfred," was all Sheriff Blake had to say.

He reached past the sheriff, grasping the man by his shirt front and lifting him off the stairs.

"Keep an eye on him until I get back," Blake said.

Manfred nodded and held the man in place as the sheriff ascended the stairs and began opening the doors at the top.

When he opened the door at the end of the hall, a body rushed out, knocking the sheriff to the ground.

Manfred shoved the man in his grasp away and set his body at the bottom of the stairs. He planned to catch the man as he tried to run by.

The man was cagey. He ran halfway down the stairs and jumped over the railing. It was the same man who had tried to dance with Lottie. Manfred ran after him, the clatter of the sheriff running down the stairs echoed behind him as he hit the saloon doors and stopped on the boardwalk. The man had vanished. Buggies and wagons rolled down the street. People milled about on the walkways.

He wasn't a cursing man but having been so close to catching the man spiked his anger. "*Verflucht!*"

"Where'd he go?" Sheriff Blake asked, stopping beside him.

"I don't know. He disappeared." Frustrated, Manfred slammed his fist into the side of the saloon, cracking a board.

"Hey, don't hurt yourself. You may need that hand if we ever catch up to that coward." Sheriff Blake put a hand on his shoulder. "Come on, you need sleep if you plan to watch the boarding house again tonight."

He wasn't going to fight the lawman. He did need sleep. And he would be at the boarding house tonight standing watch.

Lottie Mae was in the kitchen helping Belle put away the breakfast dishes when there was a knock on the front door.

"I'll get it!" called Liesa, who had been reading in the parlor. Within minutes, she flew into the kitchen. "Lottie Mae, there's a man here to see you."

"You didn't let a stranger into this house, did you?" Her fear for them all threw her caution to the wind as she marched down the hallway to the parlor.

Rounding the parlor door, she said, "Thomas you cannot—" Her mouth fell open at the sight of Mr. Pendergast, the superintendent. "I'm so sorry, I-well I thought you were someone else."

The man smiled. "With that tone, you should do a wonderful job keeping students in their place as the new teacher in Shady Gulch. We need you to start today as Mrs. Beal has had her hands full dealing with all grades after Miss Walker left."

The happiness fluttering in her chest tipped her lips into a smile. "I'd be delighted to start today." She stopped short. Not only did she need to let Beau know, but that would mean someone would have to keep an eye on the school while she was there.

"Wonderful. If you get your things, I'll escort you to the school and introduce you to Mrs. Beal," Mr.

Pendergast said.

"Yes, of course. I was helping with chores. Why don't you go on over? I'll be there as soon as I can. Your offer took me by surprise. I didn't know I'd be starting this soon." She walked him to the front door.

"You'll be along soon? I'd like to catch the train back to Bismarck." He stopped at the door, studying her.

"Yes. I'll be along as soon as I tell Mrs. Dearling what is happening." She opened the door as Manfred wandered by. His gaze latched with hers. "Thank you, Mr. Pendergast. I'll see you in a few minutes at the school," she said loud enough for Manfred to hear.

She stood on the porch, motioning for Manfred to come to her as the man walked down the street.

"What is this about the school?" Manfred asked as he stood on the porch.

"That is the superintendent. He offered me the teaching position, but I have to start today, now."

"I will walk you over and stay with you."

"You can't sit in the room with all the children." She pulled him into the parlor. "Sit, while I tell everyone and get my hat and gloves." Lottie Mae hurried down the hall. Everyone was in the kitchen, making it easier to tell them all at once.

"But what about the saloon and that mad man out to hurt all of us?" Belle asked.

"Beau encouraged me to get this position. He'll understand. As for Thomas…" She cringed. "Manfred is waiting in the parlor to walk me to the school."

"What if he barges in there and takes you?" Darie asked, her eyes wide with fear.

"I'll find a way to deal with it." She spun to the

hallway to go upstairs and get her things. Taking the stairs, she hoped she did know how to deal with the man if he came to the school.

When she stepped out into the hallway, Belle stood by her door. She held something in her hands. "Take this. I bought it when I thought the only way to get away from my husband was to kill him."

Lottie Mae peered down at the palm-sized weapon in Belle's hand.

"It fits in a skirt pocket." She held her hand out. "It's loaded and ready."

"Why did you keep it?" She peered into her friend's troubled eyes.

"You can never trust a man."

"You even believe Beau could turn on you?" The idea was ridiculous to Lottie Mae, but the sorrow in Belle's eyes said she trusted no one in trousers.

"He is just a man. They all have a breaking point where they lash out at anyone." She shoved the pistol into Lottie Mae's skirt pocket. "Be careful."

"Thank you." She squeezed her friend's hand and hurried down the stairs, tying her bonnet strings under her chin.

Manfred stood by the front door. "Are you ready?"

She nodded. Today, would be a turning point in her life. One which would get her back to the life she had before the attack. If she could find a way to rid the town of Thomas.

Chapter Twenty-five

Manfred escorted Lottie Mae to the school. He moved the two benches in the cloak room together in front of her school room door and lay down. Anyone going into her room would have to crawl over him.

He woke to the sound of giggles. Children stood in the school room doorway watching him. He rubbed a hand over his face and realized he'd not shaved as the whiskers rasped against his hand. He sat up and motioned for the children to walk around him.

"What are you doing?" Mrs. Beal asked, following her class out of the other room.

Lottie appeared in her doorway. "I'm sorry, Mrs. Beal. I didn't have time to explain this morning."

Manfred stood. "Mrs. Beal, I am Manfred Albrecht. Lottie Mae and I will be marrying soon."

The woman's gaze wandered up his body to his face. "And why are you sleeping in the cloak room?"

"There is a man—"

Lottie cut in, "There isn't a threat to the children, but a man has been bothering me." She put a hand on Manfred's arm. "Mr. Albrecht is here to make sure the man stays away."

"Did you tell Mr. Pendergast this?" Mrs. Beal backed away, her eyes narrowing.

"When Mr. Pendergast offered me the teaching position, I thought Sheriff Blake had the man." She had hoped Ty had captured Thomas when he and Manfred left the boarding house. But Manfred had told her Thomas was still loose.

"I'll have to report this to Mr. Pendergast," Mrs. Beal said, walking to the door of the building. "We'll discuss this after school. Call the children in at half past twelve. I'll be back as soon as I can."

Lottie Mae's stomach churned. She was going to lose this position after only one day.

Manfred put a hand on her shoulder. "Beau will talk to them."

She shook her head. "I can't blame them. A child could get hurt."

His stomach growled. "I will go get you something to eat. Stay inside."

"I can't. I have to watch the children."

They stepped out the door and found Lark and Savannah walking toward the school house with a pail.

"How did you know?" Lottie Mae asked, when Savannah handed her the pail.

Lottie Mae drew Manfred to sit on the school steps beside her. She opened the pail.

"Lark went to the boarding house to see what was

happening and Mrs. Dearling told him you'd been offered the teaching position. He told Beau and then came home and told me. When Mrs. Dearling also said that Manfred had escorted you to the school, I figured he would need lunch as well." Savannah smiled at them.

Lottie Mae handed a sandwich to Manfred. "I won't need to worry about a lunch tomorrow. Mrs. Beal doesn't like Manfred being at the school, but especially, the reason why." She shrugged. "She fears for the children, and I can't blame her."

"Beau will talk to her and the superintendent," Savannah said. "Don't worry. You won't lose this teaching position."

Lottie Mae glanced at her pin watch. It was time to call the children in.

"Manfred, go home and sleep. I'll keep an eye on the school this afternoon and walk Lottie Mae home," Lark said.

"Are you sure?"

She'd never seen Manfred appear so weary. And it was all because of her. She patted the gun in her pocket. There had to be a way to get rid of Thomas once and for all.

"Yes, go. You will be no good tonight if you don't get sleep." She put a hand on his arm. "Go."

He nodded and lumbered across the school yard toward town. Even knowing her past and that a mad man was after her, he stayed loyal.

"Thank you, Savannah," she said, handing the pail back to her friend. "And I appreciate you hanging around the school, Lark."

Lottie Mae reached inside the school and grasped

the handle of the bell used to call the students. As Savannah bid her husband good-bye, Lottie Mae rang the bell and caught a glimpse of Thomas watching from over by the church. Her heart lodged in her throat. Not for her safety but that of her dear friend.

"Lark, escort Savannah to the Silver Dollar. Don't take her home," Lottie Mae said, as she ushered the children inside.

"What about you?" he asked, his gaze scanning the area.

"I'll be fine. I'm surrounded by children. Thomas is by the church. Don't let Savannah walk alone." She replaced the bell, ushered her two friends out of the school house, then closed and barred the door from the inside.

Pounding on the door half-an-hour later, stopped her reading to the two classes. Lottie Mae walked slowly down the aisle, through the cloak room, and unbarred the door. Mrs. Beal and Beau stood on the steps.

"I don't like this, locking children in the school house," Mrs. Beal said, glaring at her.

"It was for their protection, and they won't know they were locked in if you keep your voice down." Lottie Mae had thought working with this woman would make her a better teacher but at the moment she found the woman trying.

"I've explained to Mrs. Beal there is no need to bring this to the superintendent's attention. We hope to have this problem solved soon. The sheriff and his deputy, along with several men he deputized, are out looking for the stranger." Beau studied her.

She nodded, understanding everyone was working to keep her safe. "I was reading to the classes. Mrs. Beal if you would like to ask your class to return to their room, I'll get on with my children's studies."

Mrs. Beal gave a curt nod and marched into the room where all the students sat.

"Are you staying here?" Lottie Mae asked Beau.

"Only until Lark returns. Go teach the children." He pushed her toward the classroom.

"I wish I hadn't brought this on everyone," she said, walking into the room, not waiting for his rebuttal.

The afternoon went quickly, once they began studying addition. At the end of the day, when the students were clamoring to leave the confines of the school room, she leaned back in her chair and breathed in the chalk dust and success. It had been a long time since she remembered ending a day and knowing she had accomplished something good. Teaching the children filled an emptiness she'd grown accustom to.

Mrs. Beal entered the room. "From the sound of the happy voices, you had a good day."

Lottie Mae smiled at the woman. "I did. I've missed teaching."

"Why have you been working at the Silver Dollar if you are a teacher?" The curiosity in the woman's voice caught her off guard.

"It's a long story that has to do with the man the sheriff is looking for." She stood, tied on her bonnet, and picked up her grade book. "I'll see you tomorrow."

Lark leaned against the cloak room wall. He eased away from it as she walked out of the classroom. "That smile says you had a good day."

"I did. The only thing that would have made it

better would be you not waiting for me. That would mean the sheriff had Thomas." She stepped out into the sunshine and scanned the area around the church.

"We searched the buildings after I left Savannah at the saloon. Saw his footprints but not him." Lark held out his arm to her.

Lottie Mae slipped her hand through the crook of his arm and realized, until Manfred, she would not have been able to accept the reverend's arm. "Is Manfred still sleeping?"

"I hope so. He's not a night owl like the rest of us."

She knew Lark was referring to his old life before becoming a reverend and the fact everyone connected to the saloon stayed up late and could survive on less hours of sleep than most folks.

"I hope he isn't hurt by all of this," she said out loud and then wished she could take the words back.

"What do you mean by that?" Lark stopped in the alley behind the saloon and faced her.

"I don't want Thomas hurting him." She held back her fear Thomas would get his revenge and leave Manfred grieving.

"Manfred can take care of himself. And you." Lark opened the back door of the saloon and left her to walk through the back room alone.

She peeked around the blanket that hid the storeroom from the saloon area. Beau was busy filling drinks at the bar as Freedom sang to a tune Jules played on the piano and Belle and Liesa served drinks. They appeared to be getting along fine without her. She couldn't go to the house and change into her saloon dress and now that she was teaching, she couldn't stay up until two in the morning working in the saloon.

She didn't know where she belonged, but she couldn't sit in the storeroom until someone escorted her to the boarding house.

Lottie Mae stepped into the saloon and caught the attention of the men nearest the bar.

"Will you look at that," one man said.

"She's marrying Manfred. Must be breaking away from the saloon," another said.

She ignored their comments and walked through the saloon to the stairs. Up in Beau's room, she found Savannah, Darie, and Mrs. Dearling working on her wedding dress.

"Just who we needed," Savannah said. "Take off your skirt and blouse. We need to try this on you."

Lottie Mae agreed with the other three, the dress was beautiful and made her look younger than her twenty-four years. "Manfred is going to think he's marrying a child," she said, staring at her reflection in the mirror on Beau's dresser.

"He'll know he married a woman when he holds you in his arms," Mrs. Dearling said, making Lottie Mae blush, Savannah laugh, and Darie gasp.

"If you have any questions about the wedding night, you can ask either Mrs. Dearling or myself," Savannah said, helping her out of the garment.

"Why would I have questions?" She was puzzled that the two women who had been and were married would think she didn't know about the coming together of a man and woman. She'd experienced the assault and wasn't sure she could go through with such intimacy but knew Manfred's gentleness would help wash away the painful memories.

Savannah motioned for Mrs. Dearling to keep Darie busy. She led Lottie Mae over to the corner farthest from the window and the light the two were using to sew by.

"You don't need to explain or tell me anything," Lottie Mae said, glancing at the door and wishing she could flee to her room in the boarding house.

"I wouldn't dream of speakin' of anythang you don't want to hear. As God as my witness, I believe that man loves you, and he'll wait for you to be ready to receive him." Savannah's face scrunched unbecomingly. "Lark explained to me that a man who has feelin's for a woman has a harder time of controllin' his emotions when he's in the throes of…"

"I would think if he loved her, he would be more careful than a man out to hurt a woman."

Savannah's cheeks flushed a deep red. "I'm sorry. I didn't give a thought about…"

"I have. Manfred might be a big man, but he is gentle. And he understands my fears. He's been married before and will teach me all I need to know." Lottie Mae walked over to the bed and sat. Thinking about sleeping next to Manfred as husband and wife had her insides fluttering with anticipation. She didn't fear their coming together. She welcomed it, to prove to Manfred she wasn't as frail as Nina.

Chapter Twenty-six

The Silver Dollar was loud and packed with men looking for a drink and entertainment when Manfred walked through the doors at eight that night. He'd slept hard after falling onto his cot. Now cleaned up, shaved, and anxious to see how Lottie Mae's day had gone, he scanned the establishment and wondered at her absence.

Beau worked behind the bar by himself. He served drinks and moseyed down to the end. "If you're ready to start your watch, Lottie Mae, Darie, and Mrs. Dearling can go to the boarding house."

"Where are they?" he asked.

"Upstairs. I'll send Belle to get them." Beau picked up empty glasses and moved to the end of the bar where Belle had set down a tray of empty glasses.

She nodded, strode to the stairs, and ascended.

Manfred watched her knock on Beau's door, disappear inside, and then the door opened. The three other women followed her down the stairs.

He caught up to them at the blanket to the back room.

"It's good to see you," Lottie said, her eyes shining.

He smiled. "I am excited to hear about your day."

Ushering the three women ahead of him through the back room, he stopped at the door to the alley and looked out. Pete, the deputy, stood in the alley. He motioned for the women to scurry across the alley and into the boarding house.

Darie and Mrs. Dearling stopped in the kitchen. Lottie Mae grasped his hand, leading him to the parlor.

"I had forgotten what a feeling of accomplishment teaching could be," she said, sitting on the settee beside him. "The children were wonderful. Eager to learn."

Her face glowed as she told him about a couple of the boys' antics. "Mrs. Beal isn't happy with me teaching while someone wants to harm me."

"We will get him. Everyone in town knows that Sheriff Blake is looking for him. They would be *dumm kopfs* to hide the man from the law." Manfred grasped her hand. "It is good to see you so happy. Doing what you were meant to do."

"Savannah had me try on my dress for the wedding." Her cheeks darkened a lovely rose color.

"You will look beautiful because you are the most beautiful woman I have seen in my lifetime." He kissed the knuckles of the hand he held.

"I didn't realize you were such a flatterer, Mr. Albrecht," she said, pretending to draw her hand from his.

"The words I speak are not flattery, they are the

truth. They only come from my heart." He leaned closer and touched his lips to hers. The day they were man and wife could not come soon enough. He wished to hold her in his arms all night and show her how he treasured her.

She drew back slightly, stared into his eyes, and whispered, "I wish nothing more than to be with you as a wife."

The significance of her words hardened his *schwanz*. He'd not felt this strong an urge to bed a woman as he did with Lottie. Even little Nina had not set his body on fire the way the woman next to him continued to do.

"*Schatzi*, to hear those words from your lips makes me happy and hungry for you." He grasped her head and kissed her with the pent-up yearning he'd harbored for her from the first day he'd set eyes on the woman at church.

They parted, both panting, yet, closing the space once more for another kiss. He drew her close, relishing the feel of her soft body in his arms and her soft lips under his.

"I believe you are supposed to be outside," Mrs. Dearling's voice stabbed at his conscience.

He slowly released Lottie Mae and stood. "I will be outside." He brushed a hand across Lottie's cheek and walked stiffly out of the room. The cool night air would help relieve his hardened appendage.

Lottie Mae's body was on fire. From her toes to the top of her head. She didn't care that Mrs. Dearling had caught them wrapped in one another's arms, kissing as if they would die without the other. She was too surprised at her need for the man and her thoughts that she had wanted to take him by the hand and lead him up to her room.

Her hands shook as she raised one to tuck a stray strand of hair behind her ear.

"The sooner you two get married and can carry on in the privacy of your own home, the better," Mrs. Dearling said. She pivoted, and her heels clacked down the hall as she returned to the kitchen.

When her body cooled and her legs held her, she climbed the stairs to her room. She had lessons to prepare for the following day.

A rustling sound came from Belle's room. She was at work at the saloon. Had she left her window open and a bird or squirrel entered?

She opened the door and froze. The man everyone was looking for, and she never wanted to see again, stood in the room.

He grinned and started toward her. "I knew I'd get you alone again."

Her mind didn't work fast enough. She opened her mouth to scream and he lunged, knocking her to the ground, his body covering her and a hand over her mouth. "Don't you make a sound, or I'll take that little bit of a woman with us. She was tougher than she looked. I didn't expect her to live."

The lack of emotion and coldness in his eyes, stifled the scream. She didn't want this man to get his hands on Darie. She'd sacrifice herself to save Darie and Manfred.

"You're going to get us out of here without no one seeing us. Cause if someone does, I'll put a bullet through them."

She had no doubt he would.

"You understand me?" He squeezed her mouth with the hand over it.

Tears burned in her eyes at the pain, but she nodded slightly.

He slowly rolled off her, taking his hand from her mouth last. "You and me are going to go someplace where no one will find us and have a discussion," he whispered in her ear and pulled her to her feet as he stood.

"Let's go. Remember, whoever sees us gets shot." He gripped her arm tight and led her down the hall to the stairs.

She prayed Mrs. Dearling and Darie were in the kitchen. She'd take him out the front door and hope Dr. Nolan saw them but didn't interfere. There was also the possibility of the deputy being out front. But the back had Manfred and the women.

They cautiously descended the stairs. To cry out would only get people killed. She had to go along with him and hope she found a chance to get away.

A board creaked as they walked to the front door. She held her breath, hoping no one heard. At the door, Thomas turned the knob and peeked out, his grip on her arm causing her fingers to go numb.

He yanked her out and down the two steps. Instead of hurrying as she'd suspected, he linked their arms and strolled down the street.

She didn't see Pete or anyone she could say anything to. They walked through the residential district, stopping at the last house at the edge of town.

Panic squeezed her chest as another man stepped out of the darkness leading two horses.

"What took you so long? I've been holding these animals for two hours," the man said.

Relief swept through her realizing the man was neither Billy or Delmar, her other attackers.

"I didn't pay you to complain." Thomas whipped his hand out fast and knocked the man in the head with the butt of his revolver.

"You didn't—" she started.

He shoved a bandana in her mouth and tied her hands before putting her on one of the horses. He mounted, grasped the reins of her horse, and they took off across the country with little moonlight to show them the way.

Chapter Twenty-seven

Dr. Nolan came out the back door of the boarding house with Mrs. Dearling and Darie in his wake.

Manfred pushed away from the back of the saloon and strode toward them. "What's wrong?" Lottie Mae wasn't with them.

"I saw Lottie Mae and some man, arm and arm walking down the street as I returned from a house call." Dr. Nolan opened the back door to the saloon and herded him in. "When I realized it wasn't you, I knocked on the boarding house door and asked Mrs. Dearling who she was with." The doctor continued as they moved through the storeroom and into the smoky saloon.

The music stopped, along with all conversation, as their small group appeared.

Manfred was still trying to make sense of what the doctor had been saying.

"What's going on?" Beau asked, standing in front of them.

"Dr. Nolan said he saw Lottie Mae and a man headed down the street arm in arm. And she's missing," Mrs. Dearling said.

Beau crossed his arms and glared at Manfred. "What do you know?"

"Nothing. I was watching the back of the house. All I saw was these three come out the back door." His mind was trying to figure how Lottie could kiss him as if she yearned for him and then walk off into the night with someone else.

"It had to be that man. The one who threatened her!" Mrs. Dearling said.

"Where was she?" Beau asked, waving Jules over into the conversation.

"She'd left the parlor and gone upstairs. That's the last I saw of her." Mrs. Dearling stared at him. "That was after I'd parted her and this one."

Beau turned to the room. "We're closing! Everyone out!"

Jules herded the grumbling men out of the saloon and locked the door.

"Which direction did they head?" Beau asked the doctor.

"East, toward the houses."

"Doctor, would you escort the women back to the boarding house and stay with them." Beau grabbed Manfred's shoulder. "Come on. We have to find them before he harms her."

Manfred followed Beau and Jules to the street alongside the boarding house. A man staggered down the dirt pathway.

Jules caught him. "Are you drunk?"

"He hit me. I held his damn horses for two hours and he hit me," the man mumbled.

"Who?" Beau asked, grasping the man's other arm. The two men hauled the staggering one to the Sheriff's Office.

Manfred followed, unsure what to do. His heart told him Lottie was in trouble, but his mind wondered if the doctor had seen a man taking a woman or a couple on a stroll.

"What are you doing bringing drunks to my jail?" Sheriff Blake asked, sitting up in his chair.

"He claims someone hit him on the head." Beau stopped the man in front of the desk. "And Lottie Mae is missing."

The sheriff's gaze landed on Manfred. "What do you mean missing?"

Beau retold what the doctor had said.

"Who hit you on the head?" the sheriff asked the mumbling man.

"Tall fella, light colored hair, crooked nose…"

This snapped Manfred out of his pitying mood. "How did he treat the woman?"

"Couldn't see very well. They walked up, he hit me, and they and the two horses were gone when I woke up."

"They? How many?" Manfred's fists clenched. Had the three who attacked her come back for revenge?

"Just the man and woman."

"Which way did they go?" He asked.

"How could I know. I was out. He hit me with his revolver."

The blood spilling down the man's face attested to his claim.

"Get a posse together, Ty. We're going after them," Beau said.

"How are you going after them in the dark?"

The sheriff wasn't taking Lottie Mae's kidnapping as seriously as Manfred liked.

"We are going after her. Now. With or without the law." He stomped out of the building and up the street toward the livery.

Footsteps followed on his heels. He knew without glancing back it was Beau and Jules. At the livery, he woke Mr. Montgomery.

They found and saddled horses. Manfred, Beau, and Jules were headed east out of town within fifteen minutes.

"We haven't a clue where they are going." Beau said when they'd trotted their horses for twenty minutes in the dark.

"There is nowhere around here to hide," Jules said.

Thoughts of where the man could be taking Lottie and what he would do to her made it hard for Manfred to concentrate over the rage burning in his gut. "He's either taking her to a train stop or…" A thought struck him. Would Lottie Mae convince the man to go to his property north of town?

"We could split up, Jules take the railroad west, Beau go east, and I will head to a spot Lottie may have taken him." His insides twisted with dread. If she did take the man to the property where he wanted to build a house for her, and the man… He growled low in his throat. If the man hurt her, she would never want to live there.

"Where are you going?" Beau asked, stopping his horse.

"My property, north of town. Lottie has been there twice. She may have talked him into hiding there." Manfred reined his horse to the north.

"You shouldn't go alone," Beau called out.

Manfred ignored the man. He wanted to get to the spring as quickly as possible. The man had already been alone with Lottie too long for his liking.

The night air grew cooler. They had ridden out of town at a gallop, with Lottie Mae grasping the saddle horn as well as she could with her hands tied together. Thomas hadn't slowed the horses until they were winded.

Once he slowed, they'd walked over railroad tracks. They were headed north. She tried to remember what she knew of the country north of the Northern Pacific Railroad. She didn't know how far the horses had galloped. It couldn't have been as far as the next water stop or she would have noticed the lights from the station master's house.

As long as they kept riding, she didn't have to worry about Thomas hurting her. They traveled for several hours, and she began to wonder how he knew where he was going in the dark. But with the bandana in her mouth, she couldn't ask questions and liked that he seemed to have forgotten her other than his hold on her horse's reins.

She hoped the man he'd hit, awoke and told the sheriff. Beau and Manfred would be looking for her. She prayed they were able to follow their tracks. But could they do that at night? She couldn't see where they were going, how would they be able to see to follow?

Despair crept into her mind. She'd been fooling herself that her life could turn around. Her tumble to shame would haunt her the rest of her life. She should try to run and let this man kill her. It would be the only way she'd ever truly be free of her past.

Giving up seemed to be the easiest path to take. She didn't have the energy to care anymore.

A large shadow began to grow in front of them. As they drew nearer the shadow, a faint paling of the sky behind her revealed they were headed west. Could that be Manfred's property? The shadow slowly revealed trees. It had to be. But there was no reason for Manfred or anyone else to believe this was where Thomas had taken her.

Everyone would follow their tracks east.

Her shoulders slumped. So close to the people she cared about, and yet, she might as well be on the other side of the Mississippi River.

When they were hidden by the trees, Thomas dismounted, stretched, and scratched.

She'd caught a whiff of his unwashed body when he'd tackled her. The thought of him coming that close to her again made her skin crawl.

Thinking he was busy tending his horse, she attempted to kick her horse to make it take off. Unfortunately, he had his foot on her reins.

"No, you don't. You ain't going anywhere until I say you can." He pulled her off the horse by her arm.

Her legs were numb from the ride, causing her to fall to the ground at his feet.

"Get up!" He shouted, yanking her arm.

She shook her head, unable to tell him her legs wouldn't hold her.

"This better not be some trick," he said, grabbing her feet and tying them together. He then ignored her as he unsaddled the horses and made a ring of rocks to start a fire.

She wanted to curl up in a ball, fall asleep, and never wake up. Shifting her body, the weight of the pistol in her pocket tugged at her waist. She'd forgotten the weapon. If she could get her hands untied… The realization she could pull the nasty bandana out of her mouth bloomed. She rolled with her back to him and pulled the cloth from her mouth. It had wicked away all her saliva, leaving her mouth as dry and parched as the land they'd crossed.

Holding her hands in front of her mouth, she began working at the leather that tied her hands together.

Footsteps approached. She dropped her hands to the ground and held still. If he realized she worked to free herself, there was no telling what he might do.

The crunch of dirt under soles stopped and the sound of rummaging through saddlebags relaxed her tense shoulders. When the footsteps retreated, she drew her hands to her mouth and began working on the leather.

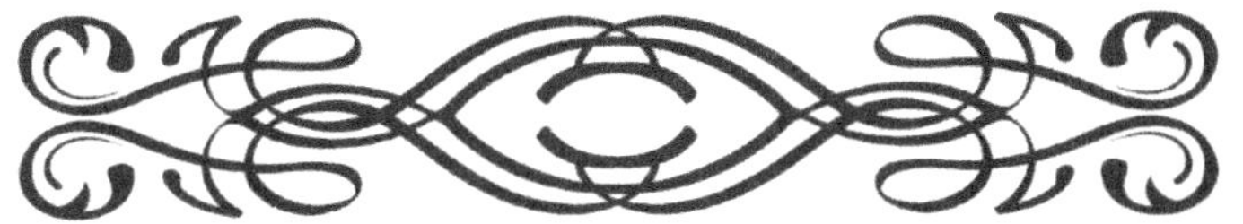

Chapter Twenty-eight

Manfred sat atop his horse as Beau checked with the station master to see if Decker and Lottie had been through here. They'd checked his property north of town at midnight and there had been no sign of the two. Beau had suggested they ride to the first station.

The sun was rising and the man out to hurt Lottie had had her in his hands for seven hours. He didn't want to think about what could have happened to her by now.

"He didn't see anyone come by here last night. They have to be holed up somewhere," Beau said, mounting his horse.

"We can't keep chasing them up and down the railroad tracks." Manfred had never felt so tired or defeated. But he wouldn't give up. Lottie Mae's life could be at stake. He would never love another if she died. He couldn't take the heartache and torment to love again.

"Let's go back to Shady Gulch and see if Ty or Jules learned anything." Beau mounted his horse, and they set the animals at a ground covering trot.

Two hours later, they arrived at Shady Gulch. "I'll go see Ty, you go on to the boarding house. Get something to eat and tell the ladies what we know." Beau continued to the depot and Manfred reined his horse down the street past his shop and on down to the boarding house.

The curtains in the parlor moved. Before he'd swung his leg over his mount to step to the ground, Freedom and Liesa stood on the porch.

"Did you find her?" Freedom asked, as he climbed the steps to the porch.

He shook his head and continued on into the building. Everyone was gathered in the parlor. Manfred stood in the doorway, his gaze taking in all the worried faces. He hoped Lottie Mae knew how much she meant to so many people.

"Beau and I checked north and east. Couldn't find them anywhere. He went to check with the sheriff and see if Jules has returned from checking west."

Mrs. Dearling stood, took him by the arm, and led him to the kitchen where she gently pushed him into a chair. "A good meal will fortify you to continue the search."

He nodded but felt as if everything was out of his control. How could he find her when they didn't know where to look?

The woman fussed around him putting a plate of ham, eggs, and potatoes in front of him along with a strong steaming cup of coffee.

He'd picked up the cup to sip when the back door flew open and Reverend Webster stepped inside. His gaze scanned the room and landed on him.

"We think we've found them," the outlaw turned reverend said, his hand on the revolver riding low on his hip.

Manfred shot to his feet. "Where?"

"Wally Richards was up north catching trout for his ma to serve in the hotel restaurant and saw a wisp of smoke coming from the spring that's on the land you bought. He made it close enough to see it was the new school teacher all tied up."

Manfred strode to the door, pushing the reverend out ahead of him. "I'll need a fresh horse."

"You can't go there by yourself," Reverend Webster argued.

"It will be easier for one person to get close. Wally showed that." He lengthened his gait to just short of a run, covering the ground quickly to the livery.

"I need a horse," he said to Montgomery.

"You ain't brought back the one you borrowed last night." Mr. Montgomery crossed his arms and stood in the livery doorway.

"It is tied up at Mrs. Dearling's boarding house." Manfred picked the man up, moved him out of the way, and grabbed the biggest, closest horse. He had the animal saddled before the livery owner or the reverend could stop him. He swung up into the saddle and set the horse at a gallop across the railroad tracks and straight for the spring.

The leather ties had become slick from Lottie Mae chewing on them, trying to loosen the knots. Frustration had her head pounding and her heart racing. Thomas would finish his breakfast soon and he'd discover she'd been working the knot loose.

There was no way to stall the inevitable, but she could continue to try and set herself free.

Footsteps approached.

A hand on her shoulder jerked her to her back.

"What are you doing?" He grabbed the wet leather and jerked her to her feet.

"Ow!" she cried out.

"You ain't very smart for a teacher. You tried to turn my family and the town against me back when I told you not to go to the superintendent. You got what was coming to you for not listening. And now you're going to get what's comin' to you for helpin' that whelp that should have died fallin' off the train and then tellin' the law what I did."

"Where's Billy and Delmar? It took three of you last time." The minute the words came out and his eyes flashed, she knew she should have remained silent.

"You just can't stay in your place." He slapped her across the face.

Her head whipped sideways from the blow, her neck popped, and her cheek stung.

"That's for bringing up those two cowards. After your big man and boss threw them out of the saloon, they tucked tail and ran." He leaned his face close. "No one is going to hear you scream out here, so there's no need to put the bandana back."

He tugged, pulling her off her feet, and dragged her across the ground.

Rocks jabbed her sides and sticks poked and scratched. She didn't call out. No one would hear, and she wouldn't give him the satisfaction of her cries.

He stopped at a tree. "I'm not ready to have my fun. I need some sleep, so I can fully enjoy showing you who's boss." He released her arms. "Stay!"

She wanted to flee but knew she'd never be able to get away with her hands and feet trussed. Instead, she chewed on the leather, watching his back as he walked over to his saddle. He picked up a rope.

Dropping her hands and her gaze, she listened rather than watched his return.

"I'll make sure you don't get no ideas while I'm sleeping." He knotted one end of the rope around the leather tying her hands together and tossed the other end over a branch of the tree. He pulled until she stood on her tip toes, her arms over her head.

"There, that should keep you from going anywhere while I sleep." He tied the rope around the tree and walked over to his belongings.

Her arms felt as if they would pop out of her shoulders. Spasms raced up and down her back muscles. She grimaced and bit her bottom lip, refusing to cry out.

Thomas rolled out a bedroll, laid down, and placed his hat over his face.

At least she didn't have to worry about him watching her. Her toes grew weary of holding her. She lowered her heels to the ground and noticed her hands slid slightly through the wet leather. The wetness had made the leather stretch. Ignoring the pain in her arms and back, she pulled steady and wiggled her hands. If she could get the strap over her thumb joint, she could slip free.

At the edge of the trees, Manfred dismounted, tying the horse to one. He walked quietly toward the spring, hoping he caught the man before he hurt Lottie. There had been a lot of hours since she was taken. A lot of harm could have been done. His fists balled, and his breathing became loud and forced. Rage turned everything he saw red. He wanted to tear the man apart with his bare hands.

The last twenty feet, he had to force his steps to be softer, quieter. Calm his breathing and ease his way to the spring.

He spotted Lottie first. She hung by her arms from a branch. A roar started in his chest and crept up his throat.

The man stirred on a bedroll twelve feet from where Lottie hung.

Manfred clenched his teeth together, holding his rage inside. He'd defeat the monster holding his woman and then free her.

His only weapon was his rage and fists. He leaped from his hiding place and raced across the short expanse to the man. As he was ready to leap on the man, Decker rolled, revolver in hand, and shot.

"No!" Lottie Mae screamed. She couldn't believe her eyes when she saw Manfred race out of the trees. But he hadn't had a weapon. Had his rage blinded him from the fact he wasn't invincible?

Her hands slid from the leather strap, dropping her throbbing arms to her side.

She groped for the pistol in her pocket.

"You big son-of-a-bitch. What made you think you could get me?" Thomas stood over Manfred, his gun pointed downward.

Blood reddened Manfred's shirt.

Lottie Mae blinked back the tears and held the pistol in both hands. The barrel was pointed at Thomas's back.

"Get away from him," she yelled.

Thomas spun, realized she was no longer hanging and pointed his revolver at her. "You can't stop me from killing him, having my way with you, and killing you."

"You will never touch me or anyone else again." She aimed and pulled the trigger. The derringer emitted a loud sound, smoke, and a bullet that lodged in Thomas's shoulder.

"You whore!" He raised his revolver.

She couldn't run, her feet were still tied. The derringer only held one bullet and she'd not been close enough to stop him.

His body crumpled to the ground and the shot hit the dirt beside her.

Manfred had rolled onto Thomas, his hands around the man's neck. "You will never lay a hand on *mien schatzi* again!"

"Manfred! No!" Lottie Mae hopped to the two men.

Thomas's hand holding the revolver hung limp.

She grabbed the weapon. "Stop! You're losing blood." Her heart stuttered to a stop at the sight of his red shirt.

Crashing of brush and horses burst into the small grassy area.

She'd never been so happy to see Beau and Jules. Ty and Pete followed behind them.

"Help! He shot Manfred." She handed the pistol to Ty and motioned for Jules and Beau to help her with Manfred.

"Doc Nolan has a buggy at the edge of the trees. We figured someone would need his help." Beau grasped Manfred under the arms and Jules took his feet. Lottie Mae quickly untied her feet and followed behind praying the bullet hadn't done as much damage as it appeared from all the blood.

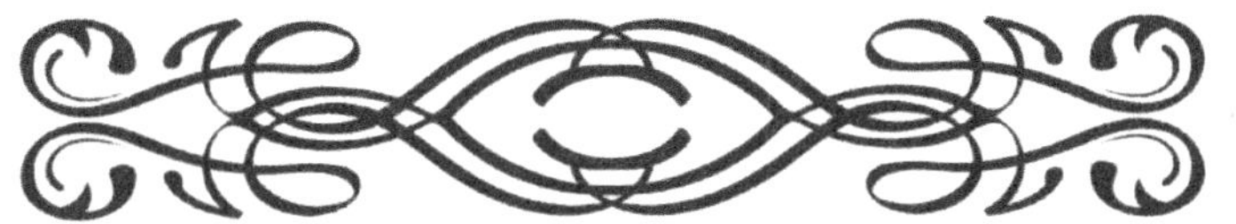

Chapter Twenty-nine

Fire like someone had stuck a hot iron in his side woke Manfred. "*Verrflucht!*" he swore.

"Manfred."

Lottie's voice tugged his eyes open.

Tears trickled down her cheeks, but she smiled.

He squeezed her small hand, resting in his. "*Schatzi*, don't cry."

"They are happy tears." She leaned down, kissing his lips.

Any other time he would have commandeered the kiss, but he barely had the energy to keep his eyes open.

She straightened. "Dr. Nolan said if the bullet had gone lower or more to the center of your body, you wouldn't be here. But we have to clean the wound and watch for infection."

He nodded and felt his eyes lowering. "The man. He is gone?" She didn't answer him. He forced his eyes open. "Is he still a threat to you?"

"No. He is no longer a threat." Lottie Mae kissed Manfred's cheek and watched his eyelids lower. She'd held his hand through Dr. Nolan removing the bullet and sewing him up. And continued to hold onto him through the day, the night, and right up until this moment when he opened his eyes.

A soft knock on her bedroom door stirred her from her somber thoughts. "Come in."

Mrs. Dearling bustled in with a tray of food. "How's the patient doing?" she asked, setting the tray on the table by the bed.

"He opened his eyes and talked to me a bit just now." She brushed the lock of hair off his forehead. She'd pondered what this man had looked like as a boy while sitting here waiting so many hours for him to wake. Now, as his face grew less pinched, more relaxed, she could almost see the little boy he'd been.

"Good. I'll take a look at his wound while you eat." Mrs. Dearling drew Lottie Mae's hand from Manfred's and tugged her out of the chair. "You're going to get sick if you don't get out and get some fresh air."

Lottie Mae wasn't concerned about herself, only Manfred. He'd nearly lost his life saving her. If he hadn't had the strength to roll himself into Thomas's legs, she was positive she wouldn't be here right now. She'd been staring down the barrel of the gun before he'd fallen.

She'd frozen in that moment, just as she'd frozen just now when Manfred asked if Thomas was gone. He was. The doctor stated her bullet had killed Thomas, but she'd seen the finger like bruises on the man's neck when the sheriff dropped the body off at Dr. Nolan's. She knew the gentle man she'd agreed to marry had killed Thomas with his bare hands.

Manfred wiggled trying to ease the pain in his side and realized he slept in a real bed. It had been years, not since Nina died and he'd headed west that he'd slept on a mattress. He hadn't realized Dr. Nolan had beds for recovery in his home.

He opened his eyes. The room was lit by a lantern. The lace curtains across the window revealed he was on the second floor. The doctor's house was only one story. He turned his head and spotted a familiar dress hanging over a chair. His heart raced. He slept in Lottie's bed.

A memory of her holding his hand, kissing him, and tears on her face came to him. A creak, had him twisting his neck and peering the opposite direction. She slept in a chair beside the bed. The bed was large enough for them both to sleep. He reached out touching her hand.

She woke. Her gaze landed on him and a smile tipped her lips. "You're awake again."

"Ja. Why do you sleep in that chair when you could lay here beside me?"

"Mrs. Dearling wouldn't be happy if she walked in and found me sleeping with you. She only allowed you in this room because she knew you were in no shape to compromise me." Her cheeks flushed.

"I am still in no shape. But I would heal faster if you rested beside me until I fall back asleep." He patted the mattress beside him.

She glanced at her pin watch. "Mrs. Dearling

doesn't usually come in until breakfast time."

Yet, she hesitated to rise out of the chair and slip beside him.

He studied her face. While she smiled, her eyes held a slight glimmer of fear. Did she fear hurting him?

"You can lay on my good side. You won't hurt me." He patted the mattress again.

A flicker in her eyes stopped his heart. "Are you having second thoughts if I would like to marry you?" As he'd ridden to the spring, he'd prayed the man hadn't hurt her. Now, staring into her eyes, he wondered if he'd been too late.

"No. Yes. I—" Tears glistened in her eyes as her hands wrung together in her lap.

"Did that man…hurt you?" He tried to lean up on his good side, but the pain kept him on his back. He shoved the pain to the back of his mind. "I do not love you less. I will not judge you for what that man did."

"He didn't hurt me. Not like that." Her hand fluttered by the side of her face. She drew it down when he studied her.

"But he hit you." He could see the darker markings on her cheek. Anger swelled in his chest.

"Yes. But you saved me from anything more. I'm grateful—"

"Grateful? You say that as if…" He couldn't continue. She made it sound as if they weren't betrothed, as if he'd helped her as he would help a stranger.

"As if what?" She leaned forward, her hands no longer wringing, her gaze on his face.

"As if you no longer care to be my wife," he said flatly. When she didn't deny it, he turned his face the other way. "I'm tired."

Several minutes passed before he heard her soft steps cross the floor, the door open, and the click of it shutting.

What had happened that she no longer felt she could be his wife? The ache of his heart surpassed the wound in his side.

It was two thirty in the morning. She couldn't wake one of the ladies to voice her concerns. She wandered out the back door, making sure she didn't make any sound to wake Mrs. Dearling, and let herself into the saloon through the back door.

Voices carried through the storeroom. Beau and Jules were discussing something in the Creole language they used when it was just the two of them. Beau told her it was the language he knew best growing up in New Orleans with Jules, his momma, and Beau's mother.

She stepped out from behind the blanket and spotted them sitting at a table, drinking coffee, and eating what looked like pie.

"Do you have another fork?" she asked.

They both glanced her way. Jules smiled and stood, walking to the bar.

Beau studied her. "Shouldn't you be up in your room watching your husband-to-be?"

She shrugged and sat.

Jules brought her a fork.

She stuck the fork into the peach pie, slipped the bite into her mouth, and chewed. Unsure where to start, she thought she'd wait for Beau to ask a question.

"How is your man?" Jules asked, instead.

"He woke up. Said his side hurts. Dr. Nolan says as long as we clean the wound twice a day, he shouldn't get an infection." She put another bite of pie in her mouth. Any other time she would savor the sweetness. Right now, she wanted to keep her mouth full and not choke, trying to swallow past the lump in her throat. A lump she'd put there herself by giving Manfred the impression she wasn't going to marry him.

"Why are you out here?" Beau put a hand on hers, stopping her from going for another bite.

Tears burned her eyes.

"You didn't lose him. He's tough. He'll be strong enough for the wedding," Beau said, patting her shoulder.

She shook her head.

"He will be strong," Jules said, nodding.

"I know he will be strong. I'm not sure I'm ready…" How had she come to be so comfortable with these two men that she could discuss her fear of marrying the man she loved?

"Not ready to marry or not ready to marry Manfred?" Beau's dark gaze peered into hers.

She hated how he seemed to know what she thought. "Him. I know that Dr. Nolan lied about how Thomas died. He didn't die from the one bullet out of that small gun I fired. I saw the bruises on his neck. Manfred killed him."

Beau and Jules exchanged glances.

Beau put his hand on hers. "Are you afraid Manfred will get so mad at you that he will hurt you?"

She nodded, even though her heart denied he'd hurt her.

"He killed Thomas to save you. And from the

blood he'd lost, the torn flesh from the bullet, I'd venture to say, he didn't have any control over his actions at that point. He was using every bit of strength he had left to save you. That is not the actions of a man who would hurt you."

Jules nodded. "He sacrificed himself for you. He would do that to himself again to keep from hurting you."

The tears in her eyes didn't sting. Her heart didn't ache. These two men had told her what she'd known in her heart but needed to get into her head.

"That man loves you so much he sacrificed himself for your safety and happiness." Beau released her hand. "You need to go back to the house."

Jules winked. "And show that man how much he means to you."

A smile spread across her face. She knew exactly how to show Manfred he was the only man for her.

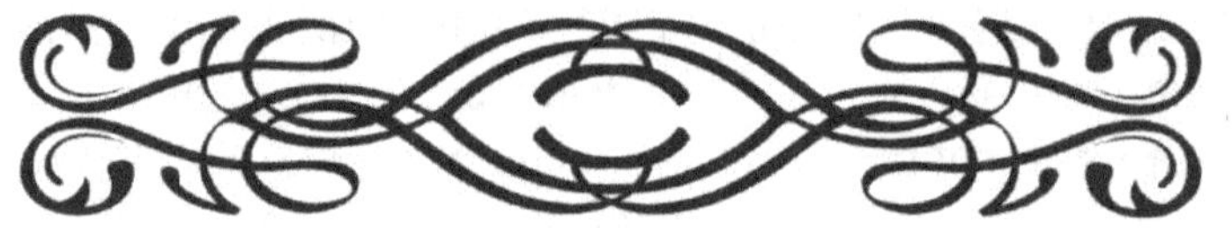

Chapter Thirty

Manfred woke from a nightmare. His heart raced and his palms were sweaty. He'd been standing at the church waiting for his bride, and Lottie Mae never walked down the aisle. Everyone left. He'd remained, waiting, until his body had turned to dust and the wind had blown it away.

Something stirred beside him. A hand slipped across his naked chest. He felt the soft press of a woman's body to his uninjured side. He turned his head and peered into the sleeping face of his *schatzi*.

He snaked his arm under her, pulling her tighter against him. She wore only her shift. He ran his hand over her curves, indulging in the softness and the shape. Her body was all woman. She kissed his neck.

"*Mien schatzi*, you tease me," he whispered and kissed her lips.

"I was tired," she said, fluttering her lashes and pressing closer, her hand across his chest, roamed down to the waistband on his drawers.

"I am in no shape to take you soaring into the clouds." He groaned as her fingertips slid under the cloth.

She leaned up on an arm, her body resting on his chest and pressed her lips to his. Lottie took charge of the kiss, dipping her tongue in to slide across his, nipping his lips, and driving him crazy.

He grasped her head in his hands, doing his best to out maneuver her.

They lay panting and staring into one another's eyes when footsteps sounded outside the door. A soft rap and someone jiggled the door knob.

Manfred laughed and whispered. "You sneak, you locked Mrs. Dearling out."

"Lottie Mae, open this door," Mrs. Dearling said.

"I will when I'm ready," Lottie replied and smiled at Manfred. "I have something I need to talk to Manfred about. Alone."

The knob rattled one more time and the footsteps faded.

"Let's get back to talking serious," he said, drawing her up and untying the string at the neckline of her shift with his mouth.

She pushed away and sat up. "I do have something I need to tell you. It's about our conversation before I showed up in your bed."

His stomach tightened, and his heart stuttered to a stop. That conversation had caused his nightmare. He studied her sitting beside him, her shift open, allowing him to see her lovely breasts for the first time, her face somber, not a hint of the playfulness of moments before.

"The one where I had the impression you didn't want to marry me?" He said the thoughts that had tumbled in his mind after her quiet departure.

She nodded. "I had some doubts. But I talked it over with Beau and Jules and they made me see my fears were foolish."

He tried to shove up to sit. The pain in his side made him grimace, but he wanted to be eye to eye with her as he asked.

"Don't. Don't sit if it hurts you." She put a hand on his shoulder.

He shook his head and continued to fight to a sitting position. Once there, he breathed in several times, ignoring the searing pain and focusing on Lottie's face. "What made you doubt my love for you?"

She hung her head. "When you asked if Thomas was gone. What did you mean?"

He studied her. She'd shot the man. Did she now regret killing him? "I wondered if your shot killed him."

She gasped.

"It's okay. I don't love you any less for killing him. He hurt you, he'd shot me, you shot him in self-defense." He reached out to pull her to him.

She didn't lean into him, but she didn't shake off his hand. "Do you remember what happened after I shot him?"

Her gaze held his. What was she trying to make him remember?

He studied her copper eyes. The events, him

charging, the shot, his side burning, and him blanking out. He'd woke to Lottie shooting the man. Decker raised a revolver aimed at Lottie. Manfred's mind snapped to his actions. He'd rolled, knocked the man down, and wrapped his hands around the man's throat.

"No!" His shout shook him out of the memory, and he peered into Lottie's eyes.

"I killed him." His shoulders slumped. He hated himself for taking a life.

The dejection and shame in Manfred's eyes tore at Lottie Mae's heart. She wrapped her arms around his head and held him to her bosom. "We both killed him. In self-defense." Her heart ached for him. Her head chastised her for bringing this piece of information out of his memory. But one day, he would have remembered. It was better now, with them both acknowledging it and moving on with their marriage.

"He would have killed us if we hadn't killed him," she said, cradling Manfred's head in her hands. His eyelids were lowered. "Look at me. Please?"

He slowly raised his lids.

She saw the pain in his heart. "I know you would never hurt or kill anyone unless my life was in jeopardy. This has shown me how much you love me." She kissed him until she felt him responding. Then she drew back and peered into his eyes. "I love you and want to be your wife from this day forward."

She leaned back, slid her shift off her shoulders and down her body. "Make love to me," she whispered, straddling his body.

Epilogue

Lottie Mae stood at the back of the church with Beau. He'd agreed to walk her down the aisle to Manfred. Her gaze was on the tall, broad-shouldered man standing next to Reverend Webster. After believing the last five years no man would ever love her and she would never be able to be a proper wife, she knew better.

Manfred had shown his love for her in so many ways. And she'd discovered that she was going to be a wife in every way. Their love making in her bed in the boarding house two weeks ago had shown her she could crave a man's touch and desire her body becoming one with his. He'd enjoyed their tryst so much, he'd ordered a big bed made and set up in the small back room of his shop. That would be their home until they built a house at the spring.

The organ music stopped. Savannah motioned from

her seat at the organ. Beau began down the aisle with Lottie Mae on his arm. Her gaze remained on Manfred's even as Beau put her hand in his.

"You are beautiful," Manfred whispered, walking her up to Lark.

The vows were exchanged, and Lark said, "You may now kiss your bride."

Manfred swept her against him, kissed her until she was out of breath, and swung her up into his arms.

Everyone laughed and cleared the way as he carried her out of the church, down the street, and straight into the room with the big bed.

About the Author

Thank you for visiting Shady Gulch. I hope you enjoyed reading about the lives of the women and men of this small railroad town. Lottie Mae and Manfred are second couple from the Silver Dollar Saloon who will fell in love. Watch for more heartwarming stories set in Shady Gulch with the women of the Silver Dollar Saloon as the heroines.

If you liked **Lottie Mae**, please leave a review. It is the best way to let an author know you enjoyed their book.

All my work has Western or Native American elements in them along with hints of humor and engaging characters. My husband and I raise alfalfa hay in rural eastern Oregon. Riding horses and battling rattlesnakes, I not only write the western lifestyle, I live it.

I love to hear from fans. You can find or contact me at:
patyjag@gmail.com
or my website – www.patyjager.net

Thank you for purchasing this Windtree Press publication. For other books of the heart, please visit our website at www.windtreepress.com.

For questions or more information contact us at info@windtreepress.com.

Windtree Press
Hillsboro, OR

www.ingramcontent.com/pod-product-compliance
Lightning Source LLC
Chambersburg PA
CBHW070626170726
48291CB00003B/899